# Through the Storms

Through the Storms: A Journey of Faith, Hope and Perseverance

Through the Storms: A Journey of Faith, Hope, and Perseverance
© 2025 The Cozy Scratchpad

Scripture quotations are taken from the King James Version (KJV) of the Holy Scriptures.

This is a work of inspirational Christian fiction. All characters, names, organizations, and events are either the product of the author's imagination or used fictitiously. Any resemblance to actual persons, living or deceased, is purely coincidental.

First Edition

Printed in the United States of America

Hardcover ISBN: 979-8-9998730-6-4

Paperback ISBN: 979-8-9998730-7-1

Published by

The Cozy Scratchpad LLC

Cleveland, Ohio

# Disclaimer

Through the Storms: A Journey of Faith, Hope, and Perseverance is a work of fiction. All characters, names, organizations, places, schools, businesses, and events are either products of the author's imagination or are used fictitiously. Any resemblance to actual persons, living or deceased, or actual locations, events, or institutions is purely coincidental.

This story includes emotionally intense themes such as trauma, grief, abuse, and a fictional account of a school shooting. These scenes are intended to reflect the emotional impact such events can have on individuals and communities. All references to schools, police departments, and local institutions are intentionally written as generic (e.g., "local school," "local police department") and are not based on any real locations or entities.

Scripture references are quoted from the King James Version (KJV) of the Holy scriptures and are included to support the spiritual message of the story. The story is not intended to offer medical, legal, or psychological advice and should not be interpreted as such.

This book is written with the goal of offering hope, healing, and awareness through fictional storytelling. Reader discretion is advised.

# Dedication

To God, Your love has been my anchor through every storm.
To my parents, for the values you instilled in me.
To my children, for being the light in my darkest moments.
To my spouse, for believing in me even when I doubted myself.
To every cousin, sibling, aunt, and uncle who has lifted me with a
call, a hug, or a word, your fingerprints are all over this book.

You are the reason I kept going.
You are my home.

With all my heart,
Kimberly

*For I know the thoughts that I think toward you, saith the Lord, thoughts of peace, and not evil, to give you an expected end.*
*Jeremiah 29:11 KJV*

# Introduction

## In the Breakroom

"How are you doing today, Cherie?" Mara asked gently as she stepped into the break room. She spotted Cherie slumped at the table, her head resting on her forearms like the weight of the world had landed there.

Cherie lifted her head slowly, eyes tired. "I've been trying to focus on the budget sheets all morning before lunch, even, but this cloudy weather isn't helping. Everything's due by the end of the day, and my brain is fogged up like the sky."

Mara poured herself a cup of coffee and sat across from her. "What's going on? You okay?"

"I'm fine," Cherie said too quickly, then sighed a long, heavy exhale that carried more than just frustration. "It's just... everybody around me is going through something. Jack's drowning in debt, my brother's about to lose his house, and to top it off, my nephew ran away last night. I'm trying to keep it together, but it's a lot."

"I hear you," Mara said, nodding. "Some days, my phone doesn't stop ringing either. One crisis call after another. But I do what I can, when I can. Sometimes, people need someone to listen."

"My ears were burning last night, literally," Cherie said with a half-smile. "Call after call for hours. I felt like a 24-hour hotline."

"You know," Mara said, sipping her coffee, "some folks do have it worse. We have to count our blessings, even when it's hard."

"You got that right," said Frederick, strolling into the break room with his Tupperware of leftovers. He moved slowly, slightly off balance, but with a quiet strength that always made people pause.

Mara raised an eyebrow and grinned. "What do you know about bad days, Fred?"

Frederick chuckled, placing his food in the microwave. "More than you think. I've had my share of rock-bottom moments. There were days I didn't know if I'd make it. But I've also seen people, real people who have climbed out of the lowest valleys and turn their pain into something powerful."

Cherie perked up, curiosity flickering in her eyes.

"Okay, Mr. Wisdom. Share some of these stories of hope, faith, and perseverance you're always talking about," Cherie said with a smirk, trying to lighten her mood.

Frederick chuckled as he stirred his coffee, but his eyes drifted just for a moment, toward the window as if searching for something long gone. When he finally spoke, his voice was softer than usual, almost reverent.

"You want to know why these stories matter to me?" he said, more to himself than to them. "Because I've seen people come back from things that should've destroyed them. Not just survive but rise. That kind of strength sticks with you."

He paused, eyes lowering slightly. "There was a time I lost everything. My family, peace of mind, and faith. I spent years blaming God for things I didn't understand. Then one day, I sat next to a man at a grief group... didn't talk much, but the weight in his eyes told me enough. He had lost his son, and the world stopped making sense to him after that. We weren't close, but I never forgot him. Never forgot the silence he sat in. Sometimes the people who say the least carry the most."

Mara and Cherie exchanged a quiet glance. The room seemed still now, the noise of the workplace muffled by something more profound.

Frederick continued, "That's why I share these stories. Not for sympathy. But because I know how it feels to be standing in the middle of a storm, wondering if the sun's ever going to rise again. And I know what it looks like when it finally does, even if it's just a sliver of light."

Then he smiled, it was small, but genuine. "So, if you're ready... I'll tell you two of those stories. It began in New York..."

## Prologue

Through the Storms is not just a collection of stories, it is a testament to the human spirit's ability to endure what was meant to break it. These pages carry the weight of grief, the ache of injustice, and the quiet triumphs that emerge from shattered places. They whisper of nights spent praying for dawn, and of hearts that keep beating long after they've been broken.

This book is for anyone who has ever felt forgotten, overwhelmed, or undone. For those navigating life after the fire, after the loss, after the betrayal. It is for the weary, the searching, and the ones still standing in the storm.

Within these stories, you'll meet people who are thrown into chaos they never asked for and somehow, find their way forward. You won't just read about survival. You'll feel the sharp edges of pain, the unexpected beauty of grace, and the relentless hope that rises when nothing else makes sense.

Storms will come, but they do not have the final word. In the wreckage, there is still faith. In the silence, there is still God. And after the winds die down, there is always the possibility of something new.

Welcome to Through the Storms, a journey of faith, hope, and perseverance.

*Book 1: From Street Work to Street Fight*

# Chapter 1

## Behind the Spotlight

Oh boy, here we go again," Jewels mumbled under her breath as the man walked in. He was short, overconfident, and trying too hard to impress her with his cologne and empty charm. She faked a smile, more out of habit than interest.

The hotel room was dimly lit, with peeling wallpaper and the lingering stench of smoke and old regrets. She sat on the edge of the bed, her eyes drifting toward the cracked windowpane. Outside, the city buzzed with life, but inside, she felt lifeless.

I can't do this anymore, she thought, her mind spinning. But I still have rent due.

The man spoke casually, oblivious to her detachment. He laughed at his jokes, took off his jacket, and assumed a closeness that made her skin crawl. She nodded, pretending to be present.

Inwardly, she was somewhere else. Somewhere safer. Somewhere cleaner. She had mastered the art of detachment letting her body go numb while her heart cried out silently to a God she wasn't even sure still listened.

He whispered something she barely heard. She gave the scripted response: a sound, a smile, a lie.

Moments passed, it was awkward, brief, meaningless.

Then, it was over.

He seemed pleased with himself, adjusting his shirt and reaching for his wallet. Jewels pulled the sheet around her and offered a polite smile. "Thanks," she said softly, though the words tasted like dust.

"You're something special," he said, grinning.

She looked away. If only you knew how little I feel.

As he left, she didn't watch him go. She reached for her purse, tucked the cash away, and sat in silence.

For a moment, the noise of the world seemed to pause. Her eyes returned to the cracked glass.

God... if You're still out there... I don't want to do this forever. Please help me. Please.

Some nights felt heavier than others, and tonight was one of them. Grabbing her small duffel bag, she zipped it closed and headed out into the night.

He was awful, she thought as her heels hit the pavement. Thank God that's over.

Three blocks later, the glowing neon lights of the club came into her view, her escape, and her trap all rolled into one. Inside, the energy pulsed through the walls of the upscale gentlemen's lounge. Jewels was a headliner—always had been. Beautiful, confident, magnetic. But behind the makeup and lights, she was just tired.

"Hey, Jewels! Where'd you sneak off to?" asked Candy from across the dressing room.

Jewels waved her off. "It wasn't important," she said, trying not to let the frustration show.

Candy didn't press. She recognized that look, the one that came after a night that felt more like a transaction than a choice. She gave Jewels a knowing nod and stepped aside.

Jewels grabbed her hygiene bag and headed for the shower. The hot water washed over her like a reset button, and for a few quiet minutes, she didn't have to pretend. When she stepped out, wrapped in a towel and silent prayer, she stared at her reflection.

Two more months. Just enough to save. Then I'm gone.

She got dressed in her signature red lingerie. The one that always brought in the high rollers and stepped back onto the main floor.

Tonight, she was 23. A college junior with three years of finance classes under her belt and a dream she hadn't fully let die. If she could pull in fifty grand before the summer ended, she'd leave it all behind.

A new city. A new journey. A fresh start.

And maybe just maybe-a new chance to find herself again.

She wanted to go back and finish her degree, but after her parents died in a car accident two years ago, it has been hard for her to adjust without them. She was the only child with no brothers or sisters to depend on.

Her parents did not have life insurance, so Jewels had to start a fundraiser to get money for the cremation, and what she didn't raise through the event, the remaining funds came from the local nightclub. She started dancing two years ago, and it wasn't the lifestyle she had imagined for herself. She wanted to get out of the street life as quickly as possible.

Jewels were walking around the main floor, swaying to an upbeat tempo as Sasha was on stage. Sasha was a little older than Jewels by one or two years. Her story was similar to Jewel's; she grew up in foster care and was looking to establish a new life for herself. Jewels and Sasha were best friends, sharing the same plans to leave the strip club behind them.

Sasha grew up in a small, tight-knit community on the outskirts of the city: her parents, hardworking immigrants, instilled in her the values of perseverance and resilience. From a young age, Sasha was known for her fierce independence and determination.

Sasha performed well academically. One day, while walking home from school, Sasha returned to find several police officers and EMS units in front of their home. A neighbor rushed to Sasha's side to divert her from seeing the massacre of her mother. Her father was struggling to keep up with her mother's medical bills, so he decided to take her life rather than his own. Without other family, Sasha moved through the foster care system.

After high school, Sasha discovered her passion for cosmetology. One day, Jewels walked into the hair salon where Sasha was working part-time as a shampooer. They instantly connected.

Sasha's friendship with Jewels grew stronger over the years. They supported each other through personal and professional struggles, often finding solace in their late-night conversations about their dreams and aspirations. Sasha admired Jewels' strength and resilience, and Jewels, in turn, valued Sasha's unwavering optimism and determination.

Just then, Jewels was walking towards one of her regular clients who always asked for a private lap dance. She was in motion to head in his direction when the arm pulled her. "Hey, beautiful," said a stranger.

Jewels hated being pulled by someone she did not know, like a piece of meat. Immediately, she rolled her eyes and snatched away. She tried to walk away, but he stepped into her path, blocking her from going forward. "Hey, where are you going in a rush? I wanted to talk to you. I will pay for a good time, as he showered her with money. She signaled for Big Mike to come over to help. Jewels did not like guys who were so aggressive and uninviting. He immediately came over to her.

"What's the problem?" he said.

Oh, nothing. I'm just asking the pretty lady for a good time," said the stranger.

I don't think she wants to be bothered with you tonight, but other girls are available.

"No, I want her!" shouted the stranger, "I want her now."

He told Jewels to leave, but the stranger tried to grab her by the arm again. Big Mike immediately intervened and grabbed the man's hand. He signaled to Rico to help escort him out of the club. As they walked, the stranger was yelling and cursing at them. When they released him at the front entrance, he tried to swing at Rico, but the punch did not land. Rico quickly retaliated with a right hook to his jaw. The man fell through the door and crashed onto the sidewalk outside.

Henry, the owner, banned him from coming back to the club. Jewels was so engrossed in Big Mike and Rico throwing the guy out of the club that she did not notice Kitty had taken the high roller to a private room. She was furious and went to the bar for a shot of something substantial. "Hey Levi, can you fix me a drink, please?"

"Yes, I can. So, who got your panties in a bunch?" said Levi.

As Jewels took the shot, disregarded the question, and left the bar. She went back to the dressing room to think about what had just happened. As she was sitting at her assigned vanity, she had her hands on her forehead, thinking about wanting the fifty grand right now. She started to cry, and that's when Sasha came in to take a shower after dancing on stage. She had a wad of cash, at least a few thousand dollars. Sasha sat down next to Jewels; she had a concerned look on her face.

"What's wrong, babes?" said Sasha.

Jewels signed and said, "I'm so frustrated with this night. I left the club early, expecting a great night, but I only ended up with $500. Then, I returned to the club and was harassed by a stranger. And, by the way, Kitty took my regular lap dance guy, who, by the way, pays well. I made no money tonight, and we only have about three hours left."

"It seems like you have had a pretty crappy night, babes, but like you said, we still have three more hours left. You need to dry your tears and get back out there. We have goals. We will not be stuck in this world. I mean, it's cool for some people, but I am ready for something else, you know!" Sasha was looking with anticipation.

Jewels nodded her head and agreed with Sasha. She wiped her tears and walked back to the main floor. She was strolling as she shut the door to the dressing room, still wiping her face. "Get yourself together, girl, right now."

As she entered the floor, she noticed a large group of guys. It appeared as though it was a bachelor's party. Her eyes saw green and heard cha-ching in her ears. She approached the group with a subtle smile, not being overly eager to dance for money. Just then, one of the guys asked for a private dance. Jewels grabbed his hand and walked him to the private showroom. He was handsome and slightly tall, but not too tall. Just right as she thought, they entered the room, and Jewels instructed him to sit down on the loveseat.

She was undeniably drawn to him. Something about his presence, it was calm yet commanding. It made her want to leave an impression. As the music played, she gave it her all, moving with grace and intensity, each motion deliberate, each glance calculated. She wasn't just dancing, she was performing. And she knew he was watching her every move.

As she moved in rhythm with the beat, he shifted slightly, clearly affected by her closeness. He reached for her, a gentle touch to her thigh, but she instinctively guided his hand away. Boundaries were part of her act. Control was her power.

Jewels pivoted smoothly, now facing him. For a split second, her gaze locked with his. His eyes were the color of a cloudless sky calm, deep, almost haunting. She caught herself staring too long and silently scolded herself. Focus, she thought. You don't get attached.

Then, unexpectedly, he leaned forward and brushed a soft kiss along her collarbone. She froze for a half-beat, not from fear, but from the strange warmth it sent through her spine. Her heart skipped. Pull it together, she reminded herself, burying the flicker of emotion beneath her professional persona.

She didn't flinch. She kept moving, fluidly and confidently, as if nothing had happened. This wasn't about him, it was about making an impression and making money and making it out of this lifestyle.

When the music faded, she slowed to a graceful stop, reached for a towel, and handed it to him with a calm, practiced smile.

Then she turned and walked away without saying another word.

Before she could touch the doorknob, he said, "I'm William."

Jewels stopped in her tracks as his deep voice was as hypnotizing as his lips. She softly replied, "I'm Jewels." She placed her hand on the doorknob, and that's when he asked if he could see her outside of the nightclub. Although she was jumping up and down inside with enthusiasm, she politely replied, "We are not allowed to date guests outside the club, sorry."

"Is that so? I guess it will be my last night here," said William.

Jewels turned her back towards him with a smile on her face as she was parallel to the door. Her body was forward, but she tilted her head over her shoulder towards William and said, "Well, maybe we can work something out." He slid by Jewels and left the room. Her knees went weak, and she slid down the door to the hutch. Both hands covered her nose and mouth as she was overcome with exhilaration.

As she was getting up from the floor, she looked at the end table. It was a large amount of cash, and his cell number was written on a napkin.

At the end of the night, Jewels made it home safely. She sat on her bed to count her money before she took a shower. "What the heck? The lap dance guy left a three-thousand-dollar tip. Oh yeah, he's now my regular."

With excitement, she called Sasha. "Hey, girly! Guess what?

With a drowsy voice, "Hey, babes," said Sasha.

"I just got a $3000.00 lap dance tip."

"What? You are such a liar!" said Sasha.

"I'm not lying," said Jewels. She sent Sasha a picture of the cash spread out on the bed.

After receiving the picture from Jewels, she said, "What the heck, babes? That's a good night. See, it worked out at the end."

The girls hung up the phone. Jewels got into the shower, and afterward, she went to bed. The next morning, she got up to make some breakfast. As she sat at the kitchen island, she thought about texting William, but she didn't want to appear eager. She decided to wait another day to reach out to him.

As always, she arrived at the club at 7:00 pm to get ready for tonight's show. Sasha and Jewels were in the dressing room putting on their makeup when they heard a knock on the door. It was Henry, letting Jewels know she would be the headliner tonight. She was excited because she knew she would earn a lot of money.

She agreed, then Henry closed the door, and she went back to focusing on their conversation. "How much do you have saved, babes?" Sasha said.

I'm at thirty-five thousand dollars, and you? "I'm at thirty-eight thousand dollars," said Sasha.

"Okay, cool, we are almost there. Do you know what you are going to do?"

"Yes, I am going to cosmetology school to get my license and then open a beauty shop," said Sasha.

I'm attending school to complete the final year of my bachelor's degree in finance. Hey, I can handle your bookkeeping. I'll open a CPA firm.

"We have a plan, now let's get this money," said Sasha. As they finished getting ready for tonight's show, Sasha wore a leopard bodysuit with a low back, and Jewels had on a black lace mesh halter high slit sexy maxi dress with a thong. As they walked out of the dressing room, all eyes were on them. Sasha continued to walk on the main floor while Jewels waited for the DJ to announce the headliner.

"Welcome, everyone, tonight as we announce tonight's headliner, Jewels, to the stage," said the DJ. Jewels stood behind the curtain as the DJ played a slow, sensual song. She was in a stance, and as the curtain began to open, she stepped into the spotlight. Under the glow of neon and strobes, she was untouchable, a goddess carved in moonlight and mystery.

The pole was cold against her palm as she took her first spin, the sequins of her deep black lingerie catching the light in dazzling fragments. The audience hushed, entranced, as Jewels moved like liquid fire. She was more than just a dancer; she was a storyteller, weaving a tale of desire and defiance with every arch of her back, every slow, deliberate roll of her hips. Among the usual faces, men with loose wallets and heavy stares were putting money down the money tube as she danced.

A stranger, seated at the edge of the room, eyes shadowed but watching. Jewels locked onto him for a fraction of a second. He wasn't like the others. No leering grin, no predatory hunger. Just quiet, unwavering attention.

She climbed the pole with effortless grace, turning upside down and sliding down with controlled precision, her heart hammering harder than usual. The moment she landed, she risked another glance at the stranger; it was William.

He raised his glass, a silent toast.

Something flickered in her chest... curiosity, apprehension, infatuation, something else she couldn't name. She gave him a wink with her left eye as she spun around the pole for the last time.

The performance ended, and the applause rose like a wave, as Jewels collected her tips from the tip tube with a practiced smile. But her mind was elsewhere, tangled in the mystery of William in the dark corner.

Jewels exited the stage and headed to the dressing room. She immediately took a shower so she could catch up with William before someone else snatched his attention. She put on a white teddy with a white steer cover. She looked like a cigarette due to her long legs.

As she was heading towards the main floor, William was standing near the bathroom. She approached him from behind to tap him on the shoulder. "Hey William,"

He turned around and said, "Hey, Jewels, I was waiting for you."

"I'm here. Do you want a private dance?"

"Yes, I do, but not here!" he replied. He had a look that she couldn't resist. She immediately said, "Well, we can go to my place." He nodded. She grabbed her jacket from the dressing room to cover up the teddy.

Jewels thought that she had never taken a guy to her home; he was the first one. There was something in his eyes, and she felt safe with him. As she got into her car, she prayed that he was not a psycho as she sat in the driver's seat. She waited for him to follow her out of the parking lot. She didn't live far from the club, but she usually stayed at the motel three blocks down the road.

"What are you thinking, taking this guy to your house? You don't know him. I'm going to take a picture of his license plate and send it to Sasha, just in case he kills me in my apartment," she said aloud while driving.

When they arrived at her apartment building, she parked out front instead of pulling into the underground garage. She stood by her car as he was parking across the street. He walked across the street and met Jewels. He grabbed her hand gently as she led the way inside the building.

Once inside her apartment, she poured two glasses of white Chardonnay for them. They sat down on the couch and started a conversation. Jewels was not usually interested in the guys that she slept with, but William was intriguing to her. However, William was not going to disclose too much personal information to Jewels. He was a nice guy, but he had a girlfriend.

"So, you want to tell me a little bit about yourself," said Jewels. William signed as if he did not want to talk.

"Well, we don't have to talk! We can get right into it so you can leave," she replied with an attitude. She thought that he was halfway decent compared to the other guys, but he was the same. Jewels put her glass of wine on the coffee table and grabbed his hand to direct him into the bedroom. Still with his wine in his hand, he took his last sip and set the glass on the bedside table. She took off his jacket and laid it on the corner chair. She started to unbuckle his shirt, but he stopped her.

William wanted to show her how much she meant to him, entirely, tenderly, and without rush. He gently lifted Jewel and laid her down with care, his eyes never leaving hers. Slowly, he unwrapped the small tokens she'd worn, setting them aside like precious reminders of their growing closeness.

He began to kiss her softly, brushing his lips along her neck and collarbone, tracing every inch with purpose and affection. His hands moved slowly, exploring her curves with reverence, learning the language of her body as if it were sacred.

Jewels closed her eyes and breathed him in. Every moment felt intentional like he wasn't just touching her body but honoring her soul. There was a rhythm to their connection, a silent understanding that this wasn't just passion, it was trust.

Their bodies moved together in harmony, each motion deepening their bond. William held her gently, guiding her to arch into him as soft gasps and quiet moans filled the room, not from urgency, but from being fully known and cherished.

As he cradled her legs, drawing her closer, Jewels felt something more profound than physical pleasure. She felt seen. Safe. Loved. In that moment, she didn't want it to end not because of the thrill, but because of the tenderness he'd given so freely.

After they were finished, she lay in bed for a moment before getting up, but William gently grabbed her hand to pull her into his chest. He kissed her forehead and said, "Don't get up just yet."

"What are you doing to me, William?" she said.

With a sly smirk on his face, he said, "Nothing," and kissed her again on the forehead. Minutes turned into hours, and Jewels woke up; it was nearly 1:00 am. Without moving, she reached over to find William, but he was gone. She sat up and saw an envelope on the side table. It contained a note and money. The note reads as follows:

Hey Jewels,

I had a great night, but I needed to leave. I didn't want to wake you. You looked so peaceful! I hope you'll call me, and we can get together again for dinner.

Peace Will

# Chapter 2

## Unfamiliar Territory

William Anderson was the kind of man who didn't need to try he was. Wealth followed him but never defined him. He had the tailored suits, the imported cologne, the kind of calm that made people either lean in or back away. People didn't just look at William, they noticed him, and they remembered.

But beneath his polished surface was a complicated past and a carefully curated life. After the death of his mother, something in William fractured. He abandoned law school, shut out his inner circle, and drifted from city to city. For a year, he lived in New Orleans, managing a jazz lounge owned by a distant cousin. Then in Atlanta. Then back to Charlotte.

Everywhere he went, women were drawn to him. And he let them. He dated often but never seriously, not after Mia. Not after the weight of guilt and grief convinced him he wasn't built for love.

He had secrets, secrets tied to his family's money, a quiet scandal buried in a court case he never talks about, and a brother who hasn't spoken to him in years.

But none of the women he dated made him pause.

Until Jewels.

There was something in her eyes, a fire and a sadness he recognized. When she danced, it wasn't just seduction. It was pain. Purpose. A message. And he couldn't stop watching her.

He told himself this was just another fling. Another curiosity.

But the way she laughed. The way she looked past his surface. The way she didn't need him only made him want her more.

William wasn't used to women being unpredictable.

Jewels made him nervous in a way that felt dangerously good.

The next evening, Jewels stood at her window, phone in hand, rereading William's note for the fifth time. She'd thought about texting him all day. She was torn between caution and a desire for curiosity. What if he were different? What if he were just like the rest?

Sasha had encouraged her to trust her instincts. "Text him. Don't overthink it. We don't get many chances for something real in this world, babes."

So, she did. Hey Will. Hope your day's going well. Dinner sounds nice. —Jewels.

Within minutes, he replied. Tomorrow night? I'll pick you up at 7.

She paused, thumb hovering over the screen. Finally, she sent it back. Sounds good. See you then.

The next day, she carefully prepped her tight curls, applied red lipstick, and wore a simple black dress that hugged her body without screaming for attention. She stared at herself in the mirror. No stilettos, no glitter, no stage lights. Just Jewels. Just her.

When he arrived, he was dressed in a navy blazer, white shirt, and slacks. Clean-cut. Confident. Kind eyes.

"You look beautiful," he said, holding the car door open.

"Thanks. You clean up nice, too," she said, sliding into the passenger seat.

Dinner was at a cozy rooftop restaurant that overlooked the city. Soft jazz played in the background. They ordered wine and tapas, and talked about everything like movies, childhood, and favorite foods. He avoided anything too deep, but it felt real.

"Do you dance because you love it?" he asked eventually.

Jewels hesitated, then shook her head. "I dance because it pays."

He nodded. "You're good at it. But I don't think that's who you are."

His words stunned her. No man had ever separated the dancer from the woman before.

After dinner, he drove her home. As they sat in the car, she reached for the door handle.

"Jewels."

She turned.

"I meant what I said. I'd like to see you again. But only if you want that too."

She smiled. "I do."

Back inside, she collapsed onto her bed, heart thudding. Something about William felt like sunlight breaking through fog.

Later that week, Jewels told Sasha everything. They were doing laundry at the 24-hour laundromat down the block.

"So, you like him?" Sasha asked, folding a hoodie.

"I do. But I'm scared. What if I mess this up?"

"You won't. Just don't let fear make the decisions for you."

Their dreams were closer than ever. Jewels were at $38,000. Sasha was nearly at $41,000. But with William on her mind, Jewels couldn't help but wonder if she was finally building something beyond survival.

The following weekend, William invited her to a jazz show. They danced, they laughed. He treated her like a woman, not a transaction.

And yet, she hadn't told him everything.

Not about her past. Not about the darker nights. Not about the clients she sometimes still saw.

She knew it couldn't stay hidden forever. But for now, she let herself have this. A night of music. A night of hope.

And the quiet promise of more.

# Chapter 3

## Chasing the Exit

The next night, Jewels stood in front of her closet, counting her cash with a sly smile. Another envelope from William, three thousand dollars again. She bit her lip.

"Dinner" or "something".... what is William trying to do to me? Maybe a relationship with him wouldn't be so bad, but I am so intrigued, she thought. She played it cool, but her grin gave her away. Perhaps I could entertain him for a while, but I have goals to achieve.

She tucked the money into a battered shoebox and slid it into the back corner of her closet. Eighty-eight hundred dollars in one night. She couldn't deny it, it was a good night.

After a hot shower, she slipped into bed and let herself rest, but the next morning she woke up with a decision to make.

She picked up her phone and called William.

He answered with that smooth tone she was starting to find dangerous. "Lunch? Country club? I'll pick you up in a couple of hours."

Jewels hesitated. "Alright."

Two hours later, she was dressed in a black blazer over a red blouse, a mid-length skirt, and those sparkling white bottom heels a stranger had left on her doorstep months ago. She didn't know who had sent them, but tonight, they finally had a purpose.

William pulled up in a silver expensive luxury car. The engine purred as he stepped out in a tailored brown suit. He opened the door for her with a nod and a quiet smile.

She slid into the plush leather seat. Her eyes widened at the sleek dash and scent of rich leather. She'd never ridden in anything like this.

Don't get carried away, she warned herself. Just because we had a couple of great nights doesn't mean anything. Stick to your goals.

The drive was long, an hour outside the city, winding past estates and iron gates until they reached the secluded country club. The valet opened her door before she even went for the handle.

William offered his hand. She hesitated for a breath, then took it.

The entrance of the club gleamed with marble floors and crystal chandeliers. Jewels had never seen anything like it. She wanted to hold her breath, afraid of breaking something just by standing there.

"Hi, Mr.—" the hostess started.

"My usual table, please," William said, cutting her off politely but firmly.

Jewels barely noticed. She was too focused on the velvet-lined menus, the pristine white tablecloths, and the gold silverware.

She leaned closer. "Is this… real gold?"

William smirked. "Would you believe me if I said yes?"

"No," she replied, narrowing her eyes.

But she smiled anyway.

As they sat down at a corner table, Jewels felt like she was a high roller at the casino, winning at the poker table.

Suddenly, William said, "Do you want a glass of wine with your lunch?"

No, thank you. I will take a glass of water right now!

"No problem, two glasses of water and a cup of coffee," said William. We will also start with calamari rings, please.

She thought, "What? Calamari?" She just smiled when William was ordering an appetizer. While they were waiting for the food to arrive at the table, she was sipping on the water. Suddenly, William asked, "How long have you worked at the club?"

She set her glass down and answered, "Two years." She explained her backstory to him and her future goals. He remained quiet as she was talking, and at the end, he nodded as if he understood her reasons.

"And what do you do for a living?" said Jewels.

He replied, "I work in sales and hospitality."

"You must do well to afford the expensive car and have a membership to this exclusive country club," said Jewels.

He was reserved, but he replied, "Yeah, I do quite well for myself. And the membership to the club is the company's. All employees are welcome," said William.

With a smile on her face, she said, "That's amazing; I need to work at your company."

"Well, what are your skills?" asked William.

"I have a year left for my bachelor's degree in finance. I am going to enroll, hopefully, in six months," said Jewels.

"Well, we could use a person like you in our accounting department," said William

As they ate their lunch, they continued to talk and engage with each other. Suddenly, the hostess came to the table and asked to speak with him privately. William excused himself from the table and followed the hostess to the front of the room. Jewels continued to eat her food and enjoyed the calming atmosphere.

"William, there you are!" said a woman. William became uncomfortable as she tried to put her arms around him. "What are you doing here?" he asked.

"I followed you, silly!" she said.

In a demanding tone, William said, "What? You are acting strange and unstable. We are no longer together, so why are you here? You need to leave."

"Don't do this to us! I have a surprise for you. It's in the car!" said the woman.

"I don't want it," shouted William. And he left the front entrance and returned to the dining hall.

The woman tried to follow him, but the security guard escorted her out of the country club.

The woman left with tears in her eyes as she got back into the car and drove away.

Back at the table, William sat down with a disgusted look on his face. Jewels looked at him but did not say anything. She did not want to pry as if they were together. They finished the meal and left the country club.

It was a semi-quiet ride back to the town; it appears that William was still upset from lunch. Once they arrived at her apartment, William opened the car door so she could get out. He hugged her and said, "We will be in touch." He got back into the car and drove off.

Jewels went upstairs to her apartment and began cleaning and doing laundry. "Same crap, different day," she was thinking about the day with William. She was separating the white clothing from the dark. She was thinking about calling off from the nightclub, but she needed the money. As she was sitting in the basement in an extra chair, her phone rang. It was Sasha. Hey, babes," What's going on?

"Nothing, just doing laundry in the basement, the maintenance finally fixed the washer machines." And I went on another date with William," said Jewels.

No, you did not!

Cautiously, Jewels replied, "I know…. I know, but listen, he's a nice guy. I think?"

Please be careful.

"I am always careful… sometimes, and he came to my house," said Jewels.

Okay, please be careful. Take it slow.

Jewels was nervous about answering her best friend, but she knew it was different with William. He had been at a distance from the moment he returned to the table after meeting with someone in the lobby.

"I've got to go, I'm doing laundry… I'll call you later," said Jewels. Jewels finished her laundry and headed back upstairs to her apartment. Once inside, Jewels made dinner and sat down in front of the television to watch the crime shows. It was her favorite show. A few hours later, she decided to head to bed; it was around 11:00 pm.

# Chapter 4

## The Price of Being Seen

Around 1:30 a.m., the sharp buzz of her phone on the nightstand pulled Jewels from a restless sleep. Squinting at the screen, she saw William's name.

She answered with a groggy, "Hello?"

"Hey... I know it's late," William's voice came through, low and uneasy. "But can you buzz me into your apartment?"

Jewels sat up slightly, her mind still foggy. "It's the middle of the night, William."

"I know. I'm sorry," he said, his tone edged with desperation. "I don't have anywhere else to go."

Her gut told her something was off. Every instinct warned her to keep the door closed, but against her better judgment, she pressed the buzzer.

The sound of the buzzer to the front door and the apartment door was heard clicking open. William walked in and headed upstairs to Jewel's apartment.

She was already standing inside the doorway, waiting for him to walk up the stairs. William met her with sleepy eyes and kissed her on the forehead.

"I'm sorry to wake you, but you were the only person that I wanted to spend the night with," said William.

It's okay, come inside!

Jewels led the way to the bedroom. She got back in bed while William took off his expensive suit and laid it on the corner chair next to the window.

Then he got into bed next to Jewels. He wrapped his arms around her and said, "Thank you for letting me stay here tonight."

"It's not a problem," she replied.

He kissed her again on the top of her head.

Jewels thought maybe he was kicked out of his house by his girlfriend or something. She could not believe that he had nowhere else to sleep. With all of his money, expensive suits, and cars, she realized that William was not completely honest about who he was.

They fell asleep.

The next morning, Jewels woke to the soft rhythm of William's breathing beside her.

She froze. He was still here.

That was strange. Men like him especially the kind who showed up at 1:30 a.m. usually slipped out before sunrise without so much as a text.

Careful not to wake him, she slid one leg off the bed.

"Where are you going?" William's voice broke the quiet, low but alert.

Jewels turned. "Sorry... I didn't mean to wake you."

"It's fine," he said, pushing himself up on an elbow. "I don't sleep heavy. My past life... well, it made nights hard sometimes. But last night being here with you, I actually felt safe."

Safe. The word stuck in her head.

I knew it, she thought. There's something else going on with this guy. Too perfect. Too smooth. Maybe a rough childhood? Maybe worse.

She wanted to ask but decided this wasn't the time.

"I'll be right back…. hold that thought," she said, heading to the bathroom.

When she returned, William was sitting on the edge of the bed, elbows on his knees, hands covering his face like he was trying to hide from the world.

"Okay, lover boy," she said lightly, masking her curiosity. "What was so urgent that you woke me in the middle of the night?"

He exhaled slowly. "Last night... wasn't great. I had to get out before things escalated. If I stayed, I probably would've been arrested."

Jewels' eyebrows shot up. "That bad, huh?"

"Yeah," he said, forcing a smile. "But it's over now. Thanks for letting me crash here."

"Anytime," she replied, still studying him.

He leaned back, eyes fixed on hers. "From what you've told me, I know you and Sasha have bigger goals, but… can we meet regularly? Two, maybe three times a week?"

Jewels tilted her head. "I already have one regular on Mondays and Wednesdays. Once a week is all I can do."

"We don't always have to… You know," he said, his voice softening. "Sometimes I just want to be around you."

She hesitated. "Alright. Which days?"

"Thursday and Friday."

"Didn't I just say no Fridays?"

"We can make it Friday nights after the club," he countered quickly.

Jewels gave him a look but said nothing.

"What are you thinking?" he asked.

"I'm trying to be flexible," she admitted. "But I'm usually dead tired after dancing half the night. Sundays, I don't work."

"I still want that time with you," he insisted.

Finally, she gave a slight nod. "Thursday and Friday nights it is."

He stood, slipping his shoes back on. "I'll pick you up Thursday."

"Pick me up? Where are we going?" she asked, curiosity creeping into her voice.

A slow smile spread across his face. "It's a surprise."

Something in his tone made her shiver not from excitement, but from a chill that crept up her spine.

He didn't look away as he added, almost too softly, "You'll like it. Trust me."

Jewels wasn't sure why, but she suddenly wished she had said no.

Jewels announced, "I hate surprises," as he got up and kissed her on the forehead, and he said, "I will see you on Thursday."

Jewels lay across the bed, still pondering a new regimen that she had acquired two days a week. Her life was already complex, with her dancing at the club almost every day. She needed and wanted a break. She was debating to herself about why she would agree to meet with another guy during the week, but she needed the money.

Jewels spent the rest of Sunday alone at her apartment, but when she went to the refrigerator for food, it was practically empty. She didn't want to go grocery shopping on Sunday, but she had no choice, so she got dressed and headed out the door.

As Jewels stepped out of the front door of the building, it was chilly for a Sunday evening in the Spring when she walked into the local market, a small but well-stocked grocery store on the corner of her street. She thought that the weather would break soon, and she couldn't wait for the warm weather. She pulled out her shopping list, tucked into the pocket of her oversized hoodie, and grabbed a cart.

She needed the essentials, such as milk, eggs, and some fresh fruit. As she strolled through the aisles, she enjoyed the familiar hum of quiet chatter and soft music playing from the store's speakers. It was one of those errands she didn't mind, a small break from the chaos of her busy week.

Jewels reached for a box of granola bars when she noticed someone standing at the end of the aisle, watching her.

A man, maybe in his early forties, dressed in an expensive-looking coat, his dark eyes studying her too intently. She ignored him at first, shaking off the discomfort, but as she moved to the next aisle, he followed.

She pretended not to notice. Maybe the man was looking for something on the same shelf. But when she turned to head toward the frozen foods, he stepped in front of her.

"Excuse me, miss," the man said, his voice smooth but unsettling. "Could I have a moment of your time?"

Jewel's heart thudded. She gripped her shopping cart tighter and took a small step back. Her mind raced was this one of those overly friendly strangers she'd had to deal with at the club. Maybe even someone who'd seen her at the club. It wouldn't be the first time she'd been followed.

"I'm kind of busy," she said politely but firmly, hoping he'd take the hint.

He didn't. Instead, he pulled a wad of cash from his coat pocket and gave her a knowing look. "I'm willing to make it worth your while," he said, his tone low and deliberate.

Jewels felt her stomach twist. Here we go, she thought. Another one who thinks he can buy whatever he wants.

She narrowed her eyes. "Why are you approaching me in a grocery store like this?"

The man smirked, as if expecting her reaction. "Let's just say I'm looking for someone who's... comfortable helping out in exchange for some quick money."

He stepped closer, holding the cash like bait. "It wouldn't take long. Nothing dangerous."

Jewels quickly moved her hands off the cart and crossed her arms. "Not interested," she said, stepping back.

He closed the gap again. "I only need thirty minutes of your time," he said in a way that made her skin crawl.

That was it. Jewels raised her voice—loud enough for nearby shoppers to hear. "NO."

Heads turned. She seized the moment, grabbed her cart, and started to push away.

There was something off about this man—too confident, too rehearsed. She glanced toward the cashier and the security cameras overhead. A shiver ran through her. Encounters like this were becoming too frequent, too risky. Without family to fall back on, she knew she couldn't afford for things to go wrong.

"Sorry," she said as she maneuvered around him. "Not interested."

He didn't take the hint. Even as she walked away, his voice followed her, offering more money, raising the amount like it was an auction. "How about four thousand?" he called out. "We could talk somewhere else. My place. No motels."

Jewels kept walking, her grip tightening on the cart. She refused to look back.

But as she turned down the next aisle, her eyes widened, he was there again, blocking her path.

"I'm not interested!" she snapped, her voice sharper now as she stepped around him.

He didn't move at first, just stood there watching her. Then a strange smile crept across his face, his expression darkening for the briefest moment before he slid the money back into his coat.

"Suit yourself," he murmured.

And just like that, he turned and disappeared into the next aisle.

Jewels exhaled a shaky breath she hadn't realized she'd been holding. Without hesitation, she pushed her cart toward the checkout, her heart pounding. She didn't know who he was or what he really wanted and she didn't care. All she knew was that no amount of money was worth the risk of finding out.

# Chapter 5

## Stalked

As soon as she checked out from the grocery store, Jewel walked as fast as she could back to her apartment. When she arrived home, she immediately locked the door. She couldn't shake the feeling that she had narrowly avoided something sinister.

Jewel decided to call Sasha to let her know what had happened at the store. She pulled out her phone, her hands still trembling slightly. She tapped on Sasha's contact, the only person who would understand just how creepy this was.

"Hey, what's up?" Sasha answered, her voice was light and cheerful.

"You will not believe what just happened to me," Jewels said, taking a deep breath.

"Okay, hold on. Why do you sound like you just saw a ghost?" Sasha's voice shifted from casual to concerned.

Jewels exhaled sharply. "Some guy at the grocery store came up to me and offered me money… for something inappropriate."

There was a long pause. "Wait… what?" Sasha finally said, her tone a mix of disbelief and anger.

"I don't know how he knew about me," Jewel continued, glancing through the curtain of her front window to double-check that she wasn't followed. "He said he needed someone 'reliable' for a favor… good time. He just kept pushing cash at me like I'd be stupid to say yes."

"Oh, no… hell no," Sasha exclaimed, her voice now alarmed. "Jewels, that sounds so sketchy! Did you tell anyone? Like, store security or something?"

Jewel sighed, rubbing her temple. "No, I just wanted to get out of there. I figured he'd leave once I walked away."

"Jewels, this situation is not normal. You should report it. What if he's done this to other women?" Sasha insisted.

Jewels swallowed. The thought unsettled her. What if he had? What if someone else had taken the money? Or worse… what if he had murdered someone before…?

"I don't know… maybe I should tell the police," she admitted.

"At least post about it in the community social media group or something," Sasha insisted. "People need to know about this guy. And don't go anywhere alone for a while, okay?"

Jewels nodded, even though Sasha couldn't see her head moving through the phone. "Yeah. Okay. I'll be careful," she said.

"You better be," Sasha huffed. "And next time, video chat me while you shop. I swear, this world is getting weirder by the day."

Jewels let out a small laugh; her nerves finally settled a bit. "Yeah, maybe I will." The feeling of hunger faded, but suddenly she heard a knock at the door.

She looked through the peephole to see who it was, but someone's hand covered it. Jewel asked, "Who is it?" There was no answer. She tried again, this time with a firm and aggressive tone, "Who is it?"

Still, no answer. She still had her phone in her hand, contemplating dialing 911, when suddenly the unknown person began kicking the door aggressively. She feared that the chain and deadbolt would break and prayed he wouldn't bust through.

A few minutes later, it stopped. Jerry from 2C came out of his apartment to see what was going on in the hallway. Jewel heard Jerry yelling at the guy.

"Hey, man, what are you doing banging on the door?" Jerry shouted. He startled the guy, who then ran off. Jewel peeked out of her door and saw Jerry standing in the hallway with a wooden baseball bat, waving it and screaming at the man as he rushed down the stairs. She opened the door to thank Jerry.

She expressed her gratitude for his help and told him about the incident at the store that had just occurred an hour earlier, which had now escalated to her front door. She mentioned that she planned to make a police report first thing in the morning, but Jerry suggested she should do it today, not in the morning. They went back inside their apartments.

Unable to eat or sleep, Jewel could not shake the situation from her mind. She couldn't believe it had escalated from the grocery store to her front door. Doing something, she rarely did, she turned on the local news. Her gut told her that something else could be happening in the neighborhood.

The screen flickered, showing the evening headlines. Suddenly, her heart stopped.

"BREAKING NEWS: Authorities are searching for a man linked to multiple disappearances in the area. A Warrant has been issued. Witnesses describe him as a well-dressed male in his forties, often seen offering large sums of money to young women in public places. If you encounter this man, do not approach or engage. Contact authorities immediately."

A picture flashed on the screen. Jewel gasped. It was him, the man from the grocery store.

Her phone slipped from her hands, hitting the floor with a thud. She started to cry and scream, then ran to the bedroom and fell on the bed. Although she hadn't met her financial goal, she was determined not to become the next victim.

She curled into the blankets, trembling. And then, a floorboard creaked in the hallway.

Jewels froze.

She wasn't alone.

# Chapter 6

## Ran

Jewels froze. The creak of the floorboard echoed like a warning in the silence. She wasn't alone. Or at least that's how it felt.

Her breath caught in her throat. For a second, she didn't move. Then, slowly, she grabbed her phone off the floor, hands shaking so hard she nearly dropped it again.

"I have to leave," she whispered, heart pounding. "It was him. The guy from the store. He's on the news. He's dangerous. He's been doing this to other women."

As the weight of her fear settled heavily on her chest, Jewel could feel her heart racing. She needed a plan, something to help her regain control. In a state of adrenaline-fueled decision-making, she grabbed her essentials, a large bag filled with her wallet, keys, clothes, and phone. She took a deep breath, reminding herself that she had to act quickly and smartly. Jewel peered through the curtain once more, half-expecting to see that familiar, dread-inducing figure lurking nearby. But the hallway was empty, the dim light casting long shadows that danced ominously against the wall.

She thought about what Sasha had said about being careful. Jewel contemplated calling her best friend back, but hesitated, unsure if she wanted to burden her with more anxiety. Instead, she quickly typed a text to Sasha, her fingers trembling as she wrote, "I saw him on the news. I'm scared, and I think I need to leave. I'll update you soon."

With one last glance at the door, she stepped away from the window and moved through her dimly lit apartment, feeling the weight of her decision as she prepared to leave. Just as she reached the front door, her phone buzzed in her hand. Jewel's heart nearly stopped as she saw Sasha's name flash across the screen.

With a mix of fear and relief, she answered. "Hello?" she said, trying to hide the quaver in her voice.

"Jewels, is everything okay? I just saw the news report!" Sasha's voice was filled with panic now. "What's going on?"

" I-I'm okay," Jewel lied, aware that her shaky breath betrayed her. "But I need to get out of here, Sasha. Can I stay with you for a little while?"

"Of course! Yes, please! Just hurry," Sasha urged. "I'm going to be waiting for you. Just drive safe, okay? You're not going to be alone in this."

With the conversation fueling her determination, Jewel quickly secured her belongings and took a deep breath. She grabbed her jacket and opened the door cautiously, peering into the hallway once more. The coast seemed clear, but her instincts screamed at her to be cautious.

She dashed down the staircase, feeling as if every sound echoed and amplified her anxiety. Every creak of the floorboards and every whisper of wind felt like a warning. Jewel hurried to her car, thankful she had parked it close; the engine roared to life, and she steered away from the building, glancing in the rearview mirror as if expecting the man to appear.

The streets were quieter than usual, and the neon lights of the storefronts blurred by as she concentrated on the road ahead. Jewel struggled to control her racing thoughts. She recalled the man's smug smile as he offered her money in the store; it felt like a nightmare that had come too close to reality.

When she finally pulled up to Sasha's apartment, her friend was already waiting by the door, a worried expression etched across her face. Jewel rushed into her friend's embrace, relief flooding through her as she breathed in the familiar scent of Sasha's perfume.

Once inside, Jewel sank onto the couch, her body shaking involuntarily. "I thought I was going to die," she whispered, tears welling in her eyes.

Sasha sat beside her, rubbing her back soothingly. "You're safe now, Jewels. We're going to figure this out together," she assured her. "If he's really dangerous, we should contact the police now and let them know that he approached you. We need to give them your information, what he looked like, everything you remember."

Taking a moment to gather her thoughts, Jewel nodded, grateful for Sasha's calm presence. They spent the next hour recounting every detail, the man's appearance, his demeanor, and the way he had offered her cash until they had everything documented. Then, with a deep breath, they dialed the police.

As the officer on the line took down the report, Jewel felt a sense of empowerment growing within her. Speaking up could prevent someone else from facing what she had. After the call ended, Jewel leaned back into the couch, feeling a mix of exhaustion and relief.

Sasha looked at her intently. "Are you going to be okay for now? You can stay here as long as you need."

"Yeah," Jewel replied softly. "I'll be okay... for now. I need to take it one step at a time."

The two friends huddled together, watching the news coverage as they waited for updates on the man from the grocery store. It was a small comfort, but one that reminded Jewel she wasn't alone. With Sasha by her side, she felt more ready to face whatever challenges lay ahead.

They vowed to keep each other safe, realizing that together they could conquer both their fears and the darkness lurking in their neighborhood. That night, Jewel slept with her phone nearby and a bolt lock installed on her friend's door, feeling a sliver of security. But deep down, she knew the battle was only beginning. And with each new day, she was determined to reclaim her sense of safety and peace.

The next morning, Jewels woke up without disturbing Sasha and went back to her apartment. Silence filled the apartment as Jewel sat with tears in her eyes and no family to reach out to besides Sasha, who had been her support system for the last two years. Then she whispered to herself, "Get out of town."

Jewels didn't need to think twice. Within an hour, she had stuffed her belongings into duffel bags and suitcases. She grabbed all of her important documents, even expensive gifts, from random guys who left items on her doorsteps or handed them to her at the nightclub. She yanked open her nightstand, grabbing the cash she kept for emergencies and the shoebox in the back of her closet where the majority of her savings were hiding. She didn't know where she was going, but she had to go.

As she threw her bags into the car and started the engine, her phone buzzed. It was a text message from Sasha. She didn't open the message. She drove out of the parking garage towards the freeway. She was going to get another cell phone once she was out of town.

As she reached the freeway, it was nearly empty, the streetlights passing in a rhythmic pattern that did little to calm Jewels' racing mind. She couldn't stop thinking about the man, his face haunting her every thought. Each mile she put between her and her past felt like a small victory, but the fear lingered.

She drove for hours, only stopping for gas and a quick bite to eat. As dawn broke, Jewels found herself on a stretch of highway surrounded by dense woods. Her eyes were heavy with exhaustion, and she knew she needed rest. Pulling into a rest area off the I-90 turnpike, she parked her car and leaned her head back, closing her eyes for just a moment.

A few hours later, realizing she had dozed off for longer than intended, she decided to freshen up in the restroom before continuing her journey.

# Chapter 7

## Who is she?

"Oh, crap, who in the world left a baby in the bathroom stall?" shouted Jewels. It was a half-clean bathroom off the I-90 turnpike. Jewels grabbed the car seat from the stall and sat the baby on the corner. "Hey, little one! With a low tone. What's your name?

Jewels were searching through the diaper bag, searching for answers. In the right pocket of the diaper bag was a folded birth certificate, a social security card, an immunization booklet, and a letter. The letter didn't have a recipient, but it contained the following message:

*"I never thought I would be writing this letter, but here I am pouring out the last of my love, my pain, and my strength onto this page before I die.*

*For so long, I have tried to be the girlfriend you needed, the mother our child deserves, and the woman who could hold everything together, even as I was falling apart inside. I've endured the loneliness, the silence, the nights spent wondering why I wasn't enough for you. And then, I found out.*

*You made a choice to break what we built, to betray the love I gave so freely. I don't know when it started or how long it's been going on, but I know this: I refuse to be second place in this relationship. I attempted to call you multiple times to tell you about your daughter, but you refused to take my calls for the last two months, so you will NEVER know her.*

*I have spent too many nights crying. The truth is, I'm leaving for good. You will never see me again, nor your daughter."*

Not yours,

Mia

Jewels thought no one could bring me to dump an infant and take my life. She should have gone to his house and slapped him. She was furious after reading the letter. She folded it and stuck it back inside the diaper bag.

Seconds later, she unfolded the birth certificate and read, "Samantha Marie Perry."

"This is insane; she's only two months," she said.

No way, no way," shouted Jewels.

Jewels thought about leaving the baby in the bathroom, but she felt guilty. She thought about how her life was already complicated, and she could barely take care of herself. She was stomping her feet on the floor like a child throwing a tantrum.

"What am I going to do with a baby?" said Jewels as she stared at Samantha's hazel eyes.

"Oh man, baby, don't look at me like that; what am I going to do?" She covered her mouth with her left hand and let out a loud moan of desperation.

"I guess we will have to figure this so-called life out together," as she grabbed the diaper bag and Samantha and headed towards her relatively new large SUV. She buckled the car seat in the backseat. After securing Samantha, Jewels got into the driver's seat and fastened her seatbelt. With her hands on the wheel, she stared out of the front window, "Lord, why do the strangest things keep happening to me? As she let out a loud sigh of distress.

"I can't do this......yes, you can do this!" she thought.

Jewels started the car and merged onto I-90 West, heading toward Illinois. By the time she reached Chicavilla, she didn't have a job lined up, but she had some money saved. She knew how to find ways to get by, but she also knew she had to be careful now especially with a baby to think about. The places she'd gone before weren't the kind she wanted to take a child into.

Her first stop was a cell phone store. She needed a new phone, but decided to keep the old one for its contact list. Once she got settled in, she planned to call Sasha and let her know where she was.

Jewels said, "I'm done with the street life in New York and I'm leaving William there, too. I need to start over. I can't keep living the way I was, especially now that I have to take care of Samantha. This baby needs me."

She pulled into the local diner on 9ᵗʰ Street. She saw the "Now Hiring" sign in the window. "Well, I have to start somewhere," said Jewels. She looked at Samantha, who was still sleeping, as she carried her inside the diner. "I have enough money for about nine months, but I know that you are going to use quite a bit of it with the price of baby formula and diapers."

As Jewels walked into the diner, she headed to the front register. "Hi, is the hiring manager available to speak with me about the waitress position?" she asked politely.

"Yeah, give me a second, and I will get him," said one of the waitresses.

Jewels sat down at the counter table with Samantha seated next to her in the empty red chair. The diner had a 1970s style with loud colors and a hippy atmosphere. She considered the restaurant charmingly adorned with wallpaper featuring 1970s music themes.

"It's not my style, but it's cute and cozy," thought Jewels. Before, Jewels had noticed the man was standing close to her, asking her name. She was so dazed from looking around the restaurant that she did not hear the man speak.

"Hello, ma'am!" said the man. "Oh, I am so sorry. I was mesmerized by the décor that I did not hear you," said Jewels. The man struck out his hand to greet Jewels.

"It's fine. Many people are captivated by it. Hi, I'm Edward." Jewels struck out her hand to greet Edward. I'm Jewels Patton.

"And who is this little darling?" said Edward. Her name is Samantha.

"How old is she? She's two months old.

"Oh, my goodness, she's gorgeous! Thank you.

"Well, can you follow me back to the office for an interview?" said Edward.

Jewels carried Samantha, who was still sleeping in the car seat, to Edward's office. "As she entered, she thought that the owner of the restaurant decorated the office with seventy themes, too." The office had a nice touch to the overall appearance of the restaurant.

"You can have a seat," said Edward. Are you new in town?

"Yes, I am. I just arrived this afternoon from New York. And I am looking for a place to stay and find work," said Jewels.

"So, you don't have a place to stay?" asked Edward.

"No, I was going to stay in the motel tonight and look for an apartment nearby," said Jewels.

Edward pulled out a travel guide with a list of affordable apartments for Jewels. You should be able to find cheap housing for now, according to the traveler's guide. "Thank you."

"Let's begin," said Edward. "Tell me a little bit about yourself."

Jewels thought, I need to make something up quick. I can't let him know about my past in New York, that I found a baby in a rest stop bathroom, and that I will probably be completely broke in a few months. What a life. She almost laughed to herself.

She smiled and said, "I'm originally from New York. I am starting over with my daughter, Samantha. It was a terrible breakup, and I am looking for a fresh start in Chicavilla."

"Why Chicavilla?" said Edward.

"Why not, Chicavilla?" said Jewels.

They looked at each other and smiled. Edward looked down at his notepad, thinking about his next question.

"Describe your experience as a server, if any?"

"I do not have any server experience, but I am a fast learner and willing to work," said Jewels.

"Ok, that's fine," said Edward.

"Do you have any professional goals?"

Yes, I am good at math. I am hoping to finish school and get my degree in finance," said Jewels.

"Wow, that's impressive. I hope that you will be able to start school soon," Edward said. Well, it's not much to waitressing, so if you want the job, then it's yours. You need to complete a background check and drug screen. This restaurant is open 24 hours a day, allowing you to choose your preferred hours. With the baby, I don't know your ideal schedule," said Edward.

"Yes, I will take it. I need to work to support my daughter. I am available to complete the background check and urine screen at any time. "I can go today," replied Jewels.

That's great. Please provide two different work schedules. What size shirt do you wear? I will give you the paperwork that you'll need.

"A small," said Jewels. Edward handed Jewels three small uniform shirts. Oh, the starting wage is $16.00 per hour and weekly pay. Can you start Monday? said Edward.

"Yes, I can," she replied.

"It will give you enough time to complete the employment requirements and find housing for yourself and your baby," he said.

Jewels stuck out her hand towards Edward. Thank you for the opportunity.

"Welcome aboard and welcome to Chicavilla!" said Edward.

Jewels left the diner and drove to a nearby motel for the night. "I'm beat, little one." Jewels paid for the room and headed towards 401-C. "I guess I need to start getting used to carrying you around."

Jewels wiped down the bathroom sink with disinfecting wipes and sprayed the bed with a cleaning spray. She sat on the bed with Samantha to change her diaper and feed her a bottle. "I need to get some wipes and diapers tomorrow. I am glad that your mother packed this diaper bag with a lot of goodies. It gives me more time to buy more stuff for you."

While Jewels was feeding Samantha, she was browsing through the traveler's guide that Edward had given her during the interview. "He was handsome, but no, Jewels! You now have a responsibility, which is Samantha! Stay focused, girl!"

She circled several affordable apartments and a couple of part-time jobs, including cleaning office buildings on weekends. "Where I go, you go!"

Jewels was constantly talking to herself and trying to keep herself encouraged. She had little to no experience raising a baby, but she knew that Samantha did not have anyone else to fight for her.

The next morning, Jewels got cleaned up and dressed to look for apartments. She viewed two unfurnished and three fully furnished apartments. She decided to sign a lease at an apartment not too far from the diner. Although it's about eighty dollars higher than the other apartments, it was closer to work, shopping, and potentially her second job. She knew that she would clean the furniture thoroughly and buy an air mattress for now until she could afford a bedroom set. She also considered visiting a second-hand store for gently used household products.

By Monday morning, her new apartment was far from perfect, but it was hers. With Samantha settled in and a few essentials in place, Jewels headed to the diner for her first day of work. "Hey, you can put the baby in the corner of the dining room. We don't use these tables. We can both keep an eye on her during our shifts," said the lady. "I'm Cassie, by the way." "Don't look too surprised; Edward has a big mouth. He told everyone that you will be starting on Monday, and you will probably bring your baby with you," she said. Edward is pretty cool, but he can't hold water.

"I see, said Jewels. I'm Jewels, and this is Samantha." We just moved here from New York.

"Oh wow, " said Cassie. I always loved to visit New York, I heard that there are a lot of street deals."

"Yeah, I am here for a fresh start.

"I hear you, girl! Change is good," said Cassie. Carol is coming in today. You'll meet her; she's a little older, so she usually works as a waitress at the bar. We can handle the floor. Oh, Tommy is coming in, too. He's nice, but he loves to gossip, so be careful what you say around him. Since this is your first day, please maintain tables five, nine, and twelve so you can be near the baby. Tommy and I will split the rest."

Jewels thought that Cassie seemed pretty friendly and helpful. "Keep your guard up, girl. Remember, you're new here," she thought.

# Chapter 8

## On the Edge

Two months later, it was a constant whirlwind of late-night feedings and diaper changes, followed by sleepless nights. She thought that single motherhood was a challenging experience. Jewels pressed the snooze button one last time before forcing herself out of bed. It was 5:00 am, and she had barely gotten four hours of sleep. The apartment was quiet except for the soft hum of the refrigerator and the rhythmic breathing of Samantha, now four months old. She tiptoed past her crib, brushing her hand lightly over her curly hair before getting ready for her first shift.

Jewels worked as a waitress at a local diner from 6:00 am to 2:00 pm, serving coffee and eggs to early risers. She had memorized the regulars' orders and always greeted them with a warm smile, though exhaustion tugged at her every movement. The tips were helpful, but they never seemed to be enough.

By the time she got home, it was enough to sleep for two and a half hours before changing into her uniform for her second job at Anderson Hotel in the Housekeeping Department from 6:00 pm to midnight. She packed Samantha's diaper bag with diapers and pre-made bottles. She headed to the door and got into her car for work.

At the diner, Samantha would sit in her car seat in a quiet corner as Jewels served the customers.

She enjoyed working at the diner; the décor was fabulous, the steady hum of the jukebox, the smell of pancakes in the morning, and she knew most of her customers by name.

As Jewels was looking around the diner to keep an eye on any refills or empty plates, she noticed an older man nursing a cup of black coffee, stirring it absentmindedly. She turned her head to the counter and saw a young woman in a leather jacket poked at her half-eaten grilled cheese. She was lost in her thoughts.

Then, the bell above the door jingled, signaling an order for table 12. Jewels quickly grabbed the food and carried it to the customer.

Suddenly, a man stepped inside, his coat dusted with rain. He was tall, maybe in his late forties, with tired eyes and a face that looked like it had seen too many long nights. As he walked towards the counter, something about him immediately caught Jewels' attention. His eyes darted around the room, his hands shoved deep into his jacket pockets. She couldn't shake the feeling that he wasn't there for a meal.

Maggie offered him a tired but polite smile. "What can I get you?"

"Money," he said. His voice was rough, like gravel scraping pavement.

"What?" Maggie's voice rose in shock.

He pulled a revolver from his jacket and pointed it straight at her. "Put all the money in a bag. Now," he barked. "Everyone, stay quiet, and don't do anything stupid!"

Gasps rippled through the diner. Chairs scraped as the man ordered everyone to the floor.

In the chaos, Jackson slipped out from the kitchen, sprinting toward the back office to alert Edward. Edward immediately grabbed the phone and dialed 911.

Jewel's heart pounded as she drove toward Samantha, scooping her up and tucking her under the table. She knelt in front of her, shielding her from sight.

At the counter, Maggie's hands trembled so badly that the bills kept slipping from her fingers.

"If you don't hurry up and stop playing games, I'm going to shoot you!" the gunman snapped.

With a shaky breath, Maggie finally shoved the last of the cash into the bag and slid it across the counter. Without another word, he snatched it and bolted out the door.

For a beat, the diner stayed frozen in silence—then the air filled with shaky sighs of relief.

Edward and the kitchen crew rushed out to check on everyone. Jewel's hands were still trembling as she pulled Samantha out from under the table and settled her back into the booth. She thought about how close they'd just come to disaster and made a quiet promise to herself: she needed another job. She couldn't risk putting her daughter in danger again.

Edward gathered the staff in the corner. "Thank you for staying calm. No amount of money is worth our lives," he said, his voice tight. "In twenty-five years, this has only happened twice." His jaw clenched. "And that's still twice too many."

A minute later, Edward's phone buzzed. He glanced at the screen. "Police said they've already identified him and will work on getting the money back. If anyone wants to go home for the day, I understand."

"I'm going to," Maggie said quietly.

"I'm pretty sure you will… You just had a gun in your face," Jackson muttered, shaking his head.

"That's fine. You were brave, Maggie. Thank you," Edward said. Everyone gave her a quick hug before she headed to the back to grab her things.

"Welcome to Chicaville, Jewels," Jackson said dryly.

Jewels gave a half-shrug.

The rest of the shift passed in a haze, adrenaline pushing them through every customer order until the lunch rush was over.

When her shift finally ended, Jewels felt the weight of exhaustion settle in. Back at home, she collapsed on the couch next to Samantha, who was already drifting into an evening nap. Jewels closed her eyes and whispered, "I guess we're working tonight, babydoll."

# Chapter 9

## The Breaking Point

The alarm clock buzzed, shaking Jewels from a shallow sleep. She forced herself up, moving through the routine she had built for herself and Samantha. Feed the baby. Dress her. Pack what they'd need. Then rush out the door toward her next job.

She clocked in at the building and wheeled a cleaning cart out of the storage closet. The cart was big enough to fit Samantha's car seat underneath, with all the cleaning products stacked neatly on top.

As she headed to the first room, scrubbing floors and wiping down mirrors, her mind drifted. She imagined a life where she didn't have to work two jobs. A life where she could read Samantha bedtime stories instead of carrying her along from shift to shift.

Some nights, she wondered if she was enough for this baby. Some days, the exhaustion was so deep she felt like she was hanging by a thread. On her worst days, she thought about leaving Samantha at the hospital or taking her to the local children's agency. She hated herself for even considering it. Chicaville was supposed to be a fresh start, but instead, she felt cornered. And no matter how tempting the quick money of her past might be, she knew it wasn't the answer anymore.

Tears welled in her eyes as she pushed the cart out of the elevator onto the second floor. She told herself she was strong, but deep down, she wasn't sure how much longer she could keep this up.

When the shift finally ended, she strapped Samantha into the backseat and started the drive home. Within minutes, the baby began to cry, it was a sharp, unrelenting sound that scraped at her nerves. Frustration boiled up inside her. She thought about pulling over at the church they were passing, maybe even... leaving Samantha there.

Then her eyes caught the words on the church sign:

I WILL STRENGTHEN YOU AND HELP YOU. — Isaiah 41:10

Her foot eased off the gas. Without really deciding, she pulled into the parking lot.

Inside, the church was quiet except for the faint hum of air conditioning. Jewels slid into the center pew, Samantha asleep in her arms, unaware of her turmoil. Tears pooled again, blurring the altar in front of her.

A shadow fell across her. "Miss, are you alright?"

She looked up to see a deacon standing beside her, his voice warm with concern.

"I'm sorry," she said quickly, wiping her eyes. "I'm just... under a lot of stress. I moved here two months ago to build a better life, but it's been so hard."

He sat down next to her. "Life isn't always peaches and cream. Some days are sweet, and other days... well, they make you want to kick, scream, shout, and cry."

A faint, humorless laugh escaped her. "I didn't think working two jobs and taking care of a baby would be this hard. I'll be twenty-four next month, and I'm still trying to take care of myself. I don't have family here just a best friend back in New York."

"It sounds like you've had to grow up fast," the deacon said gently. "You've stepped into a role that comes with a lot of responsibility protecting and providing for this child. That's not easy, but it's the right thing to do."

Jewel's gaze dropped to the baby in her lap. "This baby... she's not mine. I found her in a bathroom stall off the turnpike. Her mother just left her there. I could've walked away... but I didn't. I'm not like her."

The deacon's brows lifted. "So, you've been caring for a child you found abandoned? That's rare, Jewels. It takes a big heart to step in when someone else walks away. Do you know the story of King Solomon?"

She shook her head. "No. I've never been to church before."

"That's alright," he said. "It's worth hearing. King Solomon was a wise king who once faced a tough decision. Two women came to him both claiming to be the mother of the same baby. One of their children had died, and she accused the other of stealing her living child in the night.

"To test them, Solomon ordered that the baby be cut in half, giving each woman a part. One woman said, 'Fine, divide the child.' But the other cried out, 'Please, don't harm him give him to her instead.' Solomon knew instantly that the real mother was the one willing to give the child away to save his life."

The deacon looked at her meaningfully. "One mother abandoned her child. Another who wasn't bound by blood, chose to protect and love him. Sound familiar?"

Jewels sat in silence. "I never thought I'd be caring for someone else's baby," she said finally. "I was running from my past…"

He held up a hand. "Your past doesn't matter right now. What matters is the choices you make in the future."

She looked down, her cheeks burning.

"Lift your head, Jewels. There's no shame here."

She hesitated, then stood. "I… I can't do this anymore," she whispered. "Can you take her?"

His eyes softened, but his voice was firm. "No. But I'll make you a deal give it one more month. We have resources for single mothers here. Use them. Take all the help you need. If, after that, you still feel the same way, I'll personally help you find her a safe home. But if you don't fight for her, who will?"

She stared at him for a long moment. Then, slowly, she nodded. He handed her a stack of brochures for Financial Aid for Single Mothers, Childcare Resources Near You, and Free Parenting Workshops. They felt like lifelines, even if uncertainty still gnawed at her.

That evening, instead of going to her second job, she headed to the diner for her shift. Samantha slept in her corner spot while Jewels dove into the dinner rush.

"Hey, Jewels," Alan called.

She didn't respond, too focused on serving tables. Later, during her break, he slid into the booth across from her.

"How's motherhood treating you?" he asked.

"I'm busy right now. Please let me focus on my daughter," she said without looking up.

"Come on, don't be like that."

Her tone sharpened. "Alan, leave. Now. Or I'll tell Edward."

He stood abruptly, knocking over Samantha's bottle. Milk spilled across the table, and Jewels scrambled to save what she could.

As he walked away, he muttered an insult under his breath.

Jewels let out a slow breath, meeting her daughter's eyes. "That's the old me," she said softly. "I'm not that person anymore. I'll fight for you, baby girl. You're going to be proud of me."

# Chapter 10

## A Mother's Rage

She finished her shift and headed home. She thought about what Alan had said to her earlier, but she couldn't shake the thoughts from her mind. She knew that she was a better person now than when she was in New York. She told herself she had changed. But as the past edged closer, she began to wonder if change would be enough to keep her safe… and keep Samantha hers.

She thought about calling Sasha, but she felt guilty for leaving without notice, so she was going to wait a little while long. She hoped that she had left the street life behind and she was okay.

Jewels sat down on the couch, playing with Samantha, when her phone buzzed. It was her boss, Amanda, from her second job calling. She wanted to know if she could work at one of our subsidiary companies about thirty minutes from the city.

"I will double your pay. The hotel needed extra housekeepers on duty tonight due to an executive party that's currently taking place. I know it's last minute, but we need the help," said Amanda.

"What time do I need to be there?" she asked.

"If you can come at midnight, that would be great," said Amanda.

Jewels closed her eyes for a moment to get a little bit of rest as Samantha settled for an evening nap. As she curled up next to her on the couch, "I guess we are working tonight, babydoll."

After two hours, she was woken by the cries of Samantha as she had rolled onto the floor. She jumped up in fright, as she quickly picked her up from the floor to check for any bruises. She placed on her chest to console her from the fall patting her back as she rocked back and forth.

"You scared me, darling, I'm so sorry, I guess that I'm officially your mommy. I love you baby girl."

Jewels stood up and headed to the bedroom to rest in the bed for about an hour or so before heading out.

She arose from the bed softly to avoid waking Samantha as she put on her uniform. She looked into the mirror and thought, "I need a better first shift job." Working at the hotel is much better for Samantha and me. I'm going to ask my boss for full-time work."

She gently laid Samantha in her car seat, trying not to wake her as she headed out the door.

Once at the high-end hotel, she located Amanda, who was also there to instruct the extra cleaning staff on their assigned duties.

"I am glad that everyone agreed to work tonight. This is a big event for us, and as I mentioned on our phone call, you all will be paid extra for tonight," said Amanda.

"Candace and Joe, please take floors one, two, three, and four.

"Megan and Gwen, please take floors five, six, seven, and eight.

And Jewels and Leah, please take nine, ten, eleven, and twelve.

If anyone needs me, then I will be helping the hotel staff in the three executive conference rooms," said Amanda.

She grabbed a cart stocked with fresh linens and cleaning supplies, then rolled it toward the elevators. She had Samantha underneath the cart as always. Stepping onto the ninth floor, she was met with the scent of polished wood and expensive cologne.

Leah said tonight's rooms were on the twelfth floor, the executive suites, probably some high rollers. "I'll take the left side, and you'll take the right side. She agreed.

She took a deep breath as she started to walk down the hallway. Some nights, she dreamed of what it would be like to stay in a place like this, just once, wrapped in a bed of crisp white sheets with nothing to worry about. But in reality, she was working two jobs and caring for an infant.

Room after room, she scrubbed, changed sheets, polished mirrors, and emptied trash bins. Her body ached, but she worked efficiently, her hands moving with practiced speed.

In one of the suites, she noticed the rumpled bed sheets and evidence of a guest's late-night activities, a sight that pulled her back to memories she'd rather forget.... nights when she found herself in different hotels and motels after working at the nightclub. For a moment, the past pressed in on her, heavy and unwelcome.

Pull yourself together, she told herself silently.

"Heh," Samantha babbled from her car seat, snapping Jewels out of it. She peeled off her latex gloves, tossed them into the trash, and washed her hands thoroughly before touching the baby. Lifting her, she offered a few gentle words of comfort before changing her diaper quickly and settling her back into the car seat.

With a deep breath, Jewels returned to work. The hours passed faster than expected, and before long she found herself on the executive floor. Leah was buzzing with excitement about the possibility of spotting a high-roller guest, but Jewels wasn't interested. She wanted to finish her tasks, get home, and rest especially with their church service scheduled for the morning.

She began cleaning a suite on the right side of the hallway while Leah chatted animatedly with a hotel staff member about who might be staying in the building that night. Jewels stayed focused, but when she stepped into the hall to grab fresh towels, her gaze drifted toward the elevator. For a brief second, she caught a side view of a man stepping inside, a man who looked startlingly like William.

Her breath caught, but she quickly shook the thought away. It couldn't be. She turned back to the room and kept working.

As she pushed the cart into the storage closet, she was glad the night was over. Jewels got into her car and drove home. She was exhausted, and she pulled into the parking garage underneath the building. While in the elevator, she noticed that Samantha was missing. "Oh crap, where's Samantha?

She got out of the elevator and ran down the steps back to the parking garage. She looked in the back seat, and the car seat was not there. She was panicking. "Crap.... Crap.... crap....... I left her at the hotel in the storage room," she shouted. She jumped into the driver's seat and sped back to the hotel. As she sped down the street, she prayed that no one would take her from the storage room. "I'm so stupid. How could I have left her? I'm so sorry, Samantha. Mommy is coming…. your sorry, pitiful mother is coming."

She pulled into the roundabout directly in front of the hotel and ran inside. She went to the storage closet, glad she hadn't returned her keys to Amanda. She checked her cart, and Samantha was no longer there.

"No, no, no……oh my lord…..where's my baby?

She ran to the front to look for the night desk attendant, and no one was there. She hit the bell several times, "DINK, DINK, is anyone working tonight?" shouted Jewels.

Just then, an awkward-looking man emerged from the back office. "Hush, please stop ringing the bell. I just got her to fall asleep," said the man.

"Oh, my goodness, you have my baby?" asked Jewels. "Well, I have a baby, yes! "I'm not sure if she belongs to you. What type of mother are you to bring your baby to work, then leave her in a storage closet? I heard a baby crying from the closet as I was doing my rounds."

"Can you please give me my baby so I can go home?" Jewels asked, her voice tight.

"No. I'm calling social services to report you for child abandonment."

Without hesitation, Jewels vaulted over the counter and ran toward the office. The startled desk clerk tried to grab her arm, but she jerked it free. In that moment, she felt unstoppable like a superwoman fighting off villains.

She scooped Samantha from her car seat and held her close, pressing kisses to her cheeks. The man stormed into the office, demanding she hand the baby over.

Ignoring him, Jewels gently set Samantha back into her seat, buckled her in, and lifted the carrier onto her forearm.

"Don't mess with a mother's rage!" she shouted, blocking the doorway with her stance.

The man's jaw tightened. "Next time, don't forget your baby at work."

Her glare could have cut through steel. He froze in place, as if rooted to the floor, unable to speak another word.

Jewels walked past him, head high, and carried Samantha to the car. All the way home, she whispered apologies. "I promise to be a better mother. … give me a chance."

Once home, she ran a warm bath for both of them. Later, wrapped in a towel, Samantha lay against her chest as Jewels held her tightly, tears slipping down her cheeks.

"Please, Lord," she whispered, "help me take care of her. Let me be the mother she deserves."

After a warm bath, she fed her and rocked her to sleep. Once asleep, she lay her in the bedside bassinet. Jewels whispered again, *"Please, Lord, help me take care of Samantha. Let me be a good mother to her."*

# Chapter 11

## Turning A Page

She believed that life would get better with Samantha, but a voice from her past was about to challenge everything she'd built.

The next morning, Jewels attended church services. She got the stroller out of the SUV's trunk, put Samantha inside, and headed towards the church. Pushing the stroller, she noticed her cheeks appeared cold due to the early morning chill in the air. As she was looking down at Samantha, she said, "One more month of winter-spring air, then summer here we come."

When she entered the lower part of the church, she found an abundance of resources that she could use for Samantha, including diapers, clothing, and toys.

The deacon from a few days ago introduced himself, "I apologize for the other day. We were talking about a serious matter, and I forgot to introduce myself. I'm Malachi, one of four deacons here at the church. "I'm going to introduce Susan, our church social worker, who can help guide you in receiving county services such as supplemental food programs and search for other programs that are available."

"What are these programs?"

Malachi smiled, "Some are special supplemental nutrition programs for women with children." You can get formula and food."

Jewels widened with encouragement as she entered Susan's office. "I didn't know about these types of resources. She sat down with anticipation, eager to learn more about how to receive help and support for Samantha.

"Hi, I'm Susan Jordan.

Hello, I'm Jewels, and this is Samantha.

"I'm here to provide services for you and your baby. Let's get you signed up for programs.... Do you have your Social Security card and driver's license?

She reached into her purse and handed them to her. Then she asked for Samantha's birth certificate and social security card. Just then, she asked her if Jewels was considering adoption.

She thought, "How did she know that she wasn't mine? Oh, we don't have the same last name. Well, that's not uncommon, I think."

"You don't have to look so nervous. Malachi told me that you have a unique story. I'm just here to help," said Susan.

She nodded and smiled. "Yes, I would like to adopt her."

Great, I can start the court paperwork," replied Susan.

"How long would it take to adopt her?"

Well, it would take about three months to one year. No worries, the church will handle all attorney fees for you.

"Wow, that's great!" said Jewels.

Susan also enrolled Jewels in classes on positive parenting, financial security, and self-care at the church. She explained that a licensed social worker, therapist, or psychologist taught all of the classes. She felt better about joining the programs at the church. Slowly, Jewel's life of complications and lack of experience began to fill with community connections and resources.

She believed that life would get better with Samantha as she put her pacifier back in her mouth.

# Chapter 12

## Blood Doesn't Make the Bond

"I cannot believe that it has been a year already," said Jewels to her attorney. "Time goes by so quickly, if you are not paying attention to the time," said Jack Wallace as they sat on the court bench waiting for the judge to call their case.

Just then, the bailiff opened the door and called, "Jewels Patton." That's me as she bounced up from the bench.

Please follow me.

Jewels and Mr. Wallace entered the courtroom, escorted by the bailiff, to be seated at the front table.

Judge Walkingly cleared his throat and addressed the room. Jewels instantly became nervous. She started shaking her legs rapidly against the chair. "Please calm down, no need to be nervous. It's an adoption hearing, nothing criminal," he smiled. Jewels smirked as she calmed her legs, which had been moving.

To Jewels, this court proceeding wasn't just a formality; it was the beginning of a lifelong commitment. She had been caring for Samantha and found herself alone in a bathroom stall ten months ago. They formed a bond of mother and daughter, although Samantha is only one year old; she knows that Jewels is her mother.

"Shall we begin?" said the Judge.

Mr. Wallace stood up and said, "I am here today on behalf of Jewels Patton, who has been Samantha's caregiver for the past ten months. During this time, Jewels has demonstrated not only love and care for Samantha but also a deep commitment to providing for her future well-being. In the time Samantha has been with her, Jewels has shown her ability to meet Samantha's emotional and physical needs. She has attended all court-required appointments and has a strong, supportive network of friends who are ready to help in any way necessary."

The judge nodded and gestured for the social worker to step forward. The social worker, Ms. Jordan, stood and spoke with a gentle yet firm voice.

"Your Honor, as the supervising caseworker, I have personally visited the family several times over the past ten months. I can attest that the relationship between Jewels and Samantha is one built on trust, affection, and consistent care. Samantha is thriving in Jewels' home, and I believe finalizing this adoption will provide her with the stability and security she needs to continue to grow and flourish. I fully support this adoption."

"Thank you, Ms. Jordan. Please be seated," said the host.

Ms. Patton, do you wish to address the court with a statement before I make my decision?" said the Judge.

At first, Jewels was not going to speak, but something filled her up from the seat without hesitation. She arose and said, "Your honor, thank you for taking the time to hear this matter of adoption between Samantha Perry and me. I wanted to say that it has been hard raising a baby due to not being able to care for myself, barely. In the past, I made some decisions that weren't godly, but after finding Samantha ten months ago in a bathroom stall without anyone caring for her, I decided to take on the duties of motherhood and provide for her. With the help of the church and Ms. Jordan, I am a better person and mother. Thank you."

"Thank you, Ms. Patton, for your statement. You may be seated."

The judge took a moment to review the case file and the provided testimonies. He then looked up from the paperwork, his expression thoughtful but kind.

"After careful consideration of the evidence and the testimony from all parties involved, it is clear that Ms. Patton has shown a sincere commitment to providing Samantha with a loving and stable home. Young lady, not many people would have taken on a huge responsibility as you did. I would expect some people would have left the infant for the next person to do something or taken the baby to the nearest police station or hospital and left. Then she would have been in foster care, looking for a stable home. I applaud your commitment and dedication to Samantha Marie Perry. I am pleased to inform you, Ms. Patton, that your adoption petition has been approved. You are now Samantha's legal mother. The adoption is hereby finalized."

The sound of the gavel echoed in the courtroom, and the room erupted in applause. Jewels picked up Samantha from the stroller and hugged her tightly. Once outside the courtroom, Mr. Wallace shook Jewels' hand and said, "Congratulations." If you need anything, please don't hesitate to contact me. Good luck with everything.

Jewels said, "Thank you," and he walked away.

Ms. Jordan guided Jewels on the name change on the birth certificate and social security card across the street in City Hall. Once everything was completed, Jewels headed home with her daughter. Once home, she was looking at the new birth certificate for Samantha, which now read, "Samantha Marie Patton." She was overwhelmed with joy.

Jewels traced her finger over the new name, Samantha Marie Patton, etched into the birth certificate. The battle wasn't over, but now, Samantha was truly hers.

# Chapter 13

## One Day at a Time

The sun was beginning to rise over Chicavilla's skyline when Jewels wiped sleep from her eyes and reached for her phone. Dead. "Ugh… not again," she muttered, remembering that she'd let Samantha play games on it the night before. She forgot to plug it in.

The room was still dim and quiet except for the soft snoring coming from her daughter, curled up beside her. Jewels sat up, her muscles aching from the late shift she'd worked at the hotel. Life hadn't gotten easier, but she had gotten stronger.

Over the past couple of years, she had slowly built a new life, piece by piece, with the church's help and her unwavering determination, Jewels enrolled at the local college to pursue a degree in Finance. Mornings were for lectures, evenings for cleaning suites in the high-end hotel, and every moment in between was for Samantha, who is now 3 years old. She was juggling motherhood, education, and survival and barely keeping her balance.

"Darn it, my alarm clock didn't go off," she groaned. She scooped up Samantha and darted out the door, heels clicking against the floor as she made a mental list of everything she was already behind on.

While waiting for the elevator to go to the parking garage, she asked, "Did you turn mommy's phone off last night?" Samantha giggled as if she knew that she was in trouble.

I'm sorry, mommy. The phone died, so I set it down.

"It's okay, baby!"

She buckled Samantha into her car seat and headed towards the daycare. She thought, "I have twenty minutes to get to class. I'm going to be a few minutes late." "I have eight classes left; I can do this."

She arrived at the daycare and rushed to the door. Jewels would usually pack Samantha's bright pink backpack, but today it was left at home.  Samantha bounced excitedly through the front door, her pigtails bobbing and her chubby hands gripping her elephant. Jewels just remembered that she forgot her lunch. "Hi, Ms. Carter, I forgot Samantha's lunch and snack at home. I'm sorry we were running late this morning," she said as they entered the classroom.

"It's not a problem; it happens all the time. She will be provided a meal and snack today," said Ms. Carter.

She gave Samantha a hug and a kiss, then left the room. With two minutes to spare, Jewels walked into the classroom and sat down in the second row. She let out a sigh of relief. She thought, "It's Thursday, so I have two classes today. It's a short day." She grabbed her laptop from her bookbag and set it on the desk.

Jewels found the lecture on Business Law to be a subject both fascinating and intimidating. The professor, Dr. Simmons, was mid-sentence, explaining the differences between contract law and tort law. Jewels had taken a few business courses in the past before quitting school when her parents died, but this was her first introduction to the legal side of business.

Dr. Simmons explained that business law provides a foundational understanding for individuals pursuing business success. A contract refers to a legal agreement between two or more parties, establishing rights and obligations for those involved. When these rights or duties are not fulfilled, legal action such as lawsuits or potential bankruptcy may occur.

Dr. Simmons also outlined that there are three main types of contracts: express, implied, and unilateral. Dr. Simmons caught Jewel's eye as he looked around the room, then paused. "Let me ask you all a question," he said, drawing everyone's attention. "What's the most important aspect of a contract?"

Jewel's heart skipped a beat. She had a vague idea, but her mind was still racing through all the legal terms he had just mentioned. She glanced around, noticing that a few of the students were raising their hands. She looked down at her watch; it had been one hour and fifteen minutes, and class was wrapping up. By the time the lecture ended, Jewel's head was full of new information. She packed her things quickly and made her way out of the lecture hall. Her phone buzzed in her bag; it was the daycare. She promptly answered the phone.

"Hi, Ms. Patton, it's an emergency. Samantha is having an allergic reaction. We think it's a fish allergy. The EMS is taking her to the hospital now."

Frantically, Jewels asked, "Oh my goodness…. what hospital?"

"Chicaville General Hospital." Jewels hung up and bolted for her car. Starting the engine, she pulled out of the campus parking lot, gripping the wheel as she fought to calm herself, trying not to give in to the panic rising inside her. Samantha had never experienced any allergic reaction before, and fear gnawed at her with every passing second. The highway stretched out in front of her like an endless road, each minute feeling like an hour. Her mind raced with worst-case scenarios. She knew she had to get there…. fast.

When she finally reached the hospital, she parked as close as she could and jumped out, her hands trembling as she rushed through the lobby. At the front desk, she leaned forward, her eyes red-rimmed and voice tight.

"Can you tell me where Samantha Patton is located?"

"She's still in the emergency room. Go down the hall and to your left. She's in room 21C," said the receptionist. She pushed open the curtain and saw her daughter lying in a hospital bed with an oxygen mask over her face. "Mommy," Samantha whispered weakly.

Tears sprang to Jewel's eyes as she rushed to her side, putting her daughter's small hand in her own. "I'm here, sweetheart. You're going to be okay."

"Are you the child's mother?" said the nurse. Stiffing and crying, Jewels replied, "Yes, I am. What happened?"

"The daycare reported fish was served for lunch, and within the hour, Samantha was having trouble breathing. They immediately called

911 and still administered epinephrine while EMS arrived on the scene. She would need to stay overnight for observation."

"I didn't know that she had a food allergy," said Jewels.

It's not your fault; some allergies develop as children get older. Jewels shook her head, brushing a strand of hair from Samantha's face. "Will she be ok?"

"Yes, she will be fine. The doctor will refer you to an allergist specialist to test for other unknown allergies."

Jewels nodded as she wiped her tears.

She sat down next to Samantha's bedside. She thought, "Boy, have we been through a lot together, kiddo, but we still have to fight for each other." "I'm here.

Jewels sat by Samantha's side for hours, never leaving her, as the doctors continued to check her vitals. The relief washed over Jewels in waves, and as Samantha drifted off to sleep, safe in the hospital's care, Jewels leaned back in the chair, her heart finally at ease.

She couldn't shake the thought that she was unaware of food allergies. She needed to better prepare herself for the unexpected. She did an internet search about food allergies and ordered two books from an online bookstore about kids with food allergies. Jewels took a deep breath and said, "I can do this! We have to change our eating habits; I have to be proactive from now on and check labels."

The next morning, the nurse came into the room with the discharge paperwork for Samantha and a list of allergist specialists.

Jewels was relieved to hear that Samantha could be released from the hospital. As she carried her out, Samantha had a massive smile on her face, as if she hadn't spent the night in the hospital. Jewels buckled her in the car seat and headed home.

# Chapter 14

## Becoming More Than Enough

"You look so pretty in your graduation robe, mommy!" said Samantha. Thank you, baby!

Looking in the mirror, Jewel thought, "I can't believe that it has been two years and I'm finally graduating." Her eyes filled with tears and joy. "It took me an extra year, but I did it."

Samantha was running back and forth from her mother's bedroom to the living room. She stopped in the doorway and said, "Are we still having my birthday party on Saturday?"

"Yes, darling, we are!"

Samantha was jumping up and down, waving her arms in the air with excitement. She ran back into the living room, shouting, "I'm turning 5…..I'm turning 5."

Jewels just smiled as she finished applying her red lipstick. She got up to put on her red high heels. She shouted from the bedroom, "Are you ready to go, Sam?"

It was quiet.

"Sam."

With concern in her voice, Jewels called out, "Samantha, where are you?" As she stepped into the living room, she saw Samantha sitting on the couch with her headphones on, wholly absorbed in a game on the tablet. She gently lifted the headphones from her left ear and told her to put on her dress shoes so they could leave. Samantha slid off the couch and made her way toward the shoe rack. She plopped on the floor. "Be careful before you hurt yourself."

As she looked up at her mother, she asked, "Do you have my presents for my birthday, mommy?"

"You have to wait until Saturday."

Samantha loved to roller skate, so Jewels planned her fifth birthday celebration at the local skating and party center. The venue had it all, a dedicated party room, laser tag facilities, a skating rink, and a lively arcade area. A week earlier, Samantha had sent out invitations to all of her friends in her preschool class, excited for them to join the fun. "I'm ready to go now," said Samantha.

Jewels grabbed Samantha's hand as they walked out of the apartment and headed towards the elevator.

Once in the parking garage, Jewels unlocked the car door, and Samantha hurried over, climbing into the back seat and fastening her seatbelt.

When they arrived at the university, Jewels spotted Ms. Jordan, Malachi, and a few other church members gathered near the front entrance. Samantha darted toward Malachi and wrapped him in a hug.

"Hey, kiddo! You're getting so big," he said with a grin.

"I know," she replied proudly. "I'm turning five years old on Saturday. Are you coming to my birthday party?"

With a disingenuous look, he said, "Are you having a birthday party?"

Samantha gave a sly look, "You know that I'm having a party!!"

He tickled her under her arms and said, "Yes, I will be there, kiddo!"

Jewels thanked everyone for coming to the graduation with a sincere hug and kissed them on the cheek.

As they walked into the building, Jewels headed to the designated area for the graduates, while everyone else proceeded to the auditorium.

While standing among her college mates, Jewels had always dreamed of earning a college degree, but life had a way of getting in the way. Over the years, Jewels worked multiple jobs to support them both, but her dream never faded. It just waited.

She started to reminisce, "One evening, as she tucked Samantha into bed, she looked up at her with wide, earnest eyes. "Mom, are you going to finish school?" She remembered responding to Samantha with absolute certainty, and now she was standing in a graduation line.

She was in a daze. She continued to see vivid pictures of juggling work, parenting, and everything in between, but her dreams were still within reach if she was willing to chase them.

Tears began to fill her eyes as she thought about late nights studying after work, early mornings making breakfast, spending time with Samantha, and endless days of exhaustion. But every test she passed, every paper she turned in, brought her one step closer to the graduation stage.

"Hey, there's no crying yet," said a woman. Suddenly, Jewels was interrupted in her thoughts by another graduate student.

"I know......I know, I'm so proud of myself and my kid. It has been a long journey for both of us, but we made it," said Jewels.

"You're going to make me cry, too! I understand that there were moments when I wanted to give up because financial aid was not applied to my account on time, but the Lord made a way for me to attend class. Those are moments of gratitude and being grateful for what I have," said the woman.

Jewels also gave thanks to God for watching over her and Samantha through it all. "A few months ago, my daughter was sitting beside me while I was studying, bringing me snacks, and offering words of encouragement when I felt defeated," said Jewels. She shared how her daughter told her, "You're almost there, Mommy," her small voice filled with admiration. "It was her belief in me and God's strength that kept me going when things got tough," Jewels added.

"And now, finally, the day has arrived."

"Are you ready?"

"Yes, I am," said Jewels.

As they announced the graduates, her heart pounded with excitement. She glanced down at Samantha in a crowded auditorium, who was sitting in the third row next to Ms. Jordan.

"Jewels Anne Patton," said a school official.

As she crossed the stage to accept her diploma, the crowd cheered, but all Jewels could hear was the sound of Samantha's applause and screams. Her daughter was clapping so loudly, her face beaming with pride, and in that instant, Jewels knew that this was the most outstanding achievement of her life.

After the ceremony, Samantha ran up to her, her arms wide open. "You did it, Mommy!" she said, wrapping her arms around her.

"I couldn't have done it without you," she replied, hugging her tightly.

As they left the graduation hall together, Jewels realized that the future was full of possibilities, not just for her, but for Samantha too. And with each step they took into the next chapter of their lives, she knew that they had already achieved the most tremendous success of all: their unwavering belief in each other.

The next day, Jewels was still in disbelief. She wished that her parents were alive to see her walk across the stage. She wiped her tears and got up from the bed. The phone buzzed.

It was Amanda, her boss from work. "Good morning, Jewels.

"Good morning," she said.

"I was calling this morning to let you know about a position opening in the finance department at the hotel. I want to extend the offer to you first, as it comes with competitive pay and comprehensive benefits. You will still need to interview, but I will write a letter of recommendation," said Amanda.

"What's the title of the position?" asked Jewels.

"It's a mid-level position as a budget analyst."

Jewels did not want to sound overly eager, so she politely said, "I will apply. Thank you for calling me."

"By the way, I wanted to let you know that out of all the staff, Jewels, you are a true leader. You have the ambition and drive that we are seeking, and congratulations on completing your degree."

"Thank you so much, and I greatly appreciate it," said Jewels.

As soon as the phone call ended, she was dancing on top of her bed with excitement. "Things are looking good for us."

Moments later, Samantha came into the room to jump on the bed with her mother. "Why are we celebrating? Because of my birthday!" asked Samantha.

"Not exactly, but we can jump to celebrate your birthday. We are jumping because Mommy is going to apply for a new position at work."

"Yay, I am happy. Now I don't have to sit under the cleaning cart anymore," said Samantha.

"Jewels fell on the bed and laughed hysterically at her daughter's comment.

Why are you laughing, Mommy?"

"Because it's true, we have been through some moments, haven't we, kiddo?" said Mom.

With a massive smile on her face, Samantha replied, "Yep."

Jewels pulled her daughter close to her chest, kissed her forehead, and said, "I love you," before starting to tickle her. "Now you can sit in a chair in the office."

After the excitement was over, Jewels made breakfast for them before heading to the party store to get decorations for the upcoming Saturday party.

"I'm done," said Samantha. Jewels told her to put on a purple romper suit and sandals. As Samantha ran to her bedroom to get dressed, she cleaned up the kitchen. Then she went to her bedroom to get dressed.

Once they arrived at the party center, Samantha wanted dolls and ribbon decorations, so she went to the aisle to pick up plates, cups, napkins, and party favors.

"Do you want some candy inside the goodie bags for your friends?"

Samantha nodded with excitement.

After picking up all the decorations, Jewels headed to the Cinnamon & Grace Bakery to grab the cake. It was beautifully decorated in the shape of a doll's head.

"I love it, Mommy!" Samantha said, her eyes lighting up.

"What else do we need to get?" Jewels asked.

"I think that's it… Malachi's bringing the balloons, and Ms. Jordan's bringing the pizza, salad, and wings. I think we're all set," Mom replied.

"Okay, let's go home then," Samantha said with a grin.

"Alright, Miss Bossy!"

"I'm not being bossy," Samantha giggled. "I just want to watch TV. And besides, my party's tomorrow, so I might need to take a nap."

Jewels glanced in the rearview mirror, catching Samantha's happy little smile. She couldn't help but grin, shaking her head. That little girl, so full of personality already. She's going to keep me on my toes for the rest of my life.

# Chapter 15
## Skates and Wishes

The day had finally arrived. Samantha, with her brown curls bouncing as she jumped up and down, could hardly contain her excitement. Today was her 5th birthday, and it was going to be the best day ever.

Her mom, Jewels, had planned a special birthday party at the local skating rink, and Samantha was bursting with joy at the thought of gliding on skates with her friends.

When Jewels pulled into the parking lot, Samantha's eyes widened. The skating rink, with its shiny floors and colorful lights, looked like a castle of fun. Samantha's little hands gripped her mom's shirt as they walked inside. Jewel's hands were full of bags.

Once inside, she was directed to the private party room to start decorating while they waited for the guests to arrive.

She told Samantha to help get the party favors out of the bag while she spread the tablecloth on the table.

"Are you ready to skate, birthday girl?" asked Jewels. Samantha nodded so eagerly that her face lit up like the sun. "I've been practicing! I'm going to skate faster than anyone!" as she was placing the party favors on the table.

Mom chuckled. "We'll see about that!"

A few minutes later, Ms. Jordan showed up with the food and a gift. "Is that present for me?" said Samantha, eager to look in the bag.

"You cannot peek," said Ms. Jordan. Fifteen minutes later, Malachi brought the balloons. He decorated the room in a colorful and creative way.

Samantha's friends started to arrive and immediately wanted to wear their colorful party hats and search through the party favors.

As mom kneeled to put on Samantha's skates, she was fidgety and eager to skate. Once all laced up, she jumped up and headed for the rink.

"Please be careful, honey!"

As Jewels watched from a short distance, some of the children clung to the edge, wobbling and giggling, while others zoomed by with more skill than she had ever expected from kids their age.

Samantha found one of her friends, Ella, who was zipping around the rink, arms outstretched like a superhero.

"I can do that too!" Samantha said, and with a deep breath, she let go of the side and started to glide forward, wobbling but managing to stay upright. Her tiny legs wobbled, but her face was full of concentration.

She stayed close, cheering her on. "You're doing great, sweetie!"

Samantha's eyes sparkled. "Look, Mom, I'm doing it! I'm skating!"

As the music played, the birthday party began in full swing. The kids skated around, chasing each other and laughing. Jewels, Malachi, and Ms. Jordan watched from the sidelines, beaming with pride as Samantha's confidence grew with every lap around the rink.

"I am so proud of both of you," said Malachi.

"Me too. You all molded together perfectly," said Ms. Jordan.

"Please don't make me cry."

"We are not trying to make you cry, we are acknowledging your determination and will power to keep going even when life troubles got in the way," said Malachi. And your spiritual growth has improved. I'm proud of you. I'm so glad that we talked in the church five years ago.

"Me too, because I was ready to leave her with you, but I am glad that I didn't."

Oh, look at the time - the party is over in 30 minutes. I think that we have time for the cake and present," said Jewels.

Malachi and Ms. Jordan rallied all the kids from the rink and directed them into the private party room for cake and gift opening. The kids gathered around the table, their eyes wide with excitement as they sang "Happy Birthday" to Samantha, their voices a joyful chorus that made her heart swell.

"Make a wish, Samantha!"

Samantha squeezed her eyes shut tightly. She had so many wishes, but she knew exactly what she wanted. With a big breath, she blew out the candles, and the room erupted into cheers.

After the cake was devoured, Samantha and her friends raced back to the rink, ready for more skating.

As the party began to wind down, she looked at Samantha, who was sitting on the floor, tired but grinning ear to ear. She was covered in cake crumbs and glitter, her hair sticking out in wild curls from all the skating, but she had never looked happier.

"Samantha, you were amazing today," Mom said, brushing a strand of hair from her face.

She smiled up at her mom. "This was the best birthday ever! I can't wait to do it again next year!"

Mom laughed, scooping her into her arms. "We'll see about that, but for now, you've earned a good rest."

As they left the rink, with the lights twinkling in the distance, Samantha leaned her head on her mom's shoulder, her heart full of joy. It was a birthday she would never forget, a day when she had learned to glide, to laugh, and to make memories that would last forever.

And as they headed home, Jewels couldn't help but smile, knowing that in Samantha's eyes, her 5th birthday had been nothing short of a blessing.

# Chapter 16
## Collateral Truth

A week after graduation, Jewels arrived at the hotel with a mix of nerves and hope buzzing through her. As she stepped through the lobby, she spotted Amanda standing by her office door, waiting with a confident smile.

Jewels smiled, but anxiety entered her blood flow. She knew that getting this job would be another milestone in her life. She was encouraged by reciting, "I can do all things through Christ who strengthens me."

As Amanda opened the door to the large conference room, it was filled with massive executive chairs and a large table that would fill her entire house.

Jewels looked at the three people sitting at the table, one of whom seemed extremely familiar. "No way, is that William, she thought. "It could be"

With a nervous smile, she sat down across from the executives, and they introduced themselves as,

"Hi, Jewels, I'm Mara Henderson, Director of HR."

"Good morning, Jewels. I'm Victor LaVon, Director of Finance."

As the last person began to speak, something about him made her pause. His eyes, his voice, that smile... it all felt familiar. Crap. It's William from New York.

"Hi, Jewels, I'm William Anderson, CEO of Anderson Enterprises," he said, extending his hand.

Trying not to show any emotion, she extended her hand and smiled politely to greet each member of the interview panel.

"Let's begin," said Mr. LaVon, leaning forward. "We'll start by discussing the executive structure within the company and where the budget analyst role fits into our operations."

Jewels nodded attentively, listening as he outlined the company's departments, leadership roles, and reporting lines.

Mrs. Henderson glanced at her notes and prepared to move into the formal questions. "Alright, Ms. Patton, could you start by telling us about your background in budget forecasting and cost analysis?"

Before Jewels could answer, William raised his hand. "There's no need for an interview," he said smoothly. "I've already made my decision…. she's hired."

Mrs. Henderson blinked in surprise. "Are you certain, sir?"

Mr. LaVon's eyes flicked to her with a look that suggested she'd just stepped into forbidden territory.

William looked at Mara with a stern expression. "Yes, I received a resume and a letter of recommendation." There's no need for an interview. Thank you for your time. You all are dismissed, except for you, Jewels.

She became nervous again; she could feel sweat building under her arms, but she remained calm, without any visible facial expressions.

As everyone left the room, William did not take his eyes off of her.

When the conference room door slammed shut, William leaned over the desk, his eyes fixed on her. His tone was low but loaded.

"Why did you leave New York?"

Jewels hesitated, gripping the armrest of the chair. Just give him the short version, she told herself. He was watching her too intently, as if searching for something in her face.

Finally, she spoke. "Someone was stalking me… it scared me. I panicked and left."

William's brows drew together, his jaw tightening. "Jewels? It's been five years. I thought what we had was… something special." His voice softened, almost pleading. "I wanted to be with you."

Her eyes flicked away. Their short time together had been different, but she'd been trapped in a world she desperately wanted to leave behind. "William, our time together was brief. I was a different person back then. I needed to escape that lifestyle, and I found a way to do it. I'm sorry I left without telling you, but I had to go."

"I respect that," he said, his gaze darkening, "but you could have at least called or texted. I was furious... but I'm also relieved you're here. Safe."

She nodded faintly. "I'm sorry."

"Are you seeing anyone?" His question came out abruptly.

Her head snapped toward him. "Are you serious, William? You're asking me that now? What difference does it make? I can see the ring on your finger."

"Just answer the question," he pressed, his voice sharpening.

"No," she replied firmly. "May I go now, since you've already decided to hire me?"

"Yes, you can go," he said, pausing for a beat, "but... have lunch with me."

"It's not a good time for me."

His lips pressed into a thin line, disappointment etched in his features. "You're dismissed."

She almost fired back, but stopped herself. There was no point starting an argument. She didn't care if he was the CEO, she wouldn't tolerate anyone treating her like she was beneath them. Rising from the chair, she pushed it back in neatly and walked toward the door without a word.

But William didn't like to be ignored. He stood quickly, his footsteps closing the space between them.

As her hand touched the door handle, he slammed it shut and blocked her exit, pressing her back against it. His face was close, too close.

"William...."

He leaned in, aiming for her lips. She turned her head sharply, and his mouth brushed her cheek instead. Undeterred, he tried again, but she pushed against his chest, keeping the distance.

His frustration flared. He kissed her neck, his hand sliding down toward her blouse. She caught his wrist before he could go any further.

"Stop." Her voice was firm, unshaken. She shoved him back a step. "Those days are in the past. You're married. Go home to your wife."

Without waiting for his reply, Jewels opened the door and walked out, her pulse racing, but her head held high.

She went back to Amanda's office because she knew that there was probably gossip floating around the hotel.

"Hi, Amanda! Is everything okay? Do I get the job?" Jewels asked, stepping into the office.

"Hey, Jewels, come in." Amanda smiled knowingly. "Yes, you got the job, but… well, everyone's been curious about the connection between you two."

From the hallway, Jewels caught a faint whisper of two staff members passing by. "That's her," one murmured. "She knows the CEO."

Jewels raised an eyebrow. Here we go, she thought. "There's no connection. I met him five years ago in New York, briefly."

Amanda tilted her head. "Oh, okay….so, you two dated or something?"

"Not at all," Jewels replied, keeping her tone even. "We were introduced through mutual friends. That's it. No connection."

She could already hear the rumor mill grinding to life. Another voice from down the corridor floated in: "I bet she got the job because of him." Jewels' jaw tightened, but she refused to react. Let them talk. My work will speak for itself.

"When's my first day?" she asked, steering the conversation away.

"Oh, I just got an email from HR," Amanda said. "Please head to their office to complete your paperwork."

Jewels made her way to the HR department, where she signed the forms for her new position, an annual salary of $105,000, full medical benefits, and a retirement plan.

When everything was finalized, Mrs. Henderson congratulated her and instructed, "Report to the second floor at 8:30 a.m. on Monday."

Walking out of HR, Jewels felt a rush of excitement about the opportunity ahead. A small part of her considered apologizing to William, but she quickly decided against it, she had no interest in opening that door again.

Leaving the hotel behind, Jewels craved a calmer environment. She decided to stop by the church to volunteer for a few hours before picking up Samantha from school.

Inside, a large group of volunteers was busy packing food into boxes for the community food drive. Jewels greeted everyone with a smile and slipped into the line, grabbing boxes and filling them with canned goods and dry staples. The rhythm of the work was calming, a welcome change from the sharp glances and hushed voices she'd faced earlier.

Across the room, Malachi spotted her. "Hey, everyone," he called out over the chatter, "let's give it up for Jewels! She just got a promotion at work and graduated from the local college with a finance degree!"

The crowd broke into warm applause. Jewels froze for a moment, caught off guard. She covered her nose and mouth with both hands, cheeks flushing as every pair of eyes seemed to turn her way.

A glance at her watch told her it was time to pick up Samantha from school. She waved goodbye, thanked everyone, and headed out.

Sitting in the school's pick-up line, her mind drifted right back to the hotel. I can't believe William is the CEO of the company, she thought. And even more shocking, he tried to kiss me, knowing he's married. Shame on him. What was he thinking?

She looked toward the school entrance, spotting Samantha's class lining up to leave. Her thoughts softened. My life is good with just me and her. I'll start dating when the right guy comes along. I'm only twenty-nine, I have time for marriage… if it's even in my future.

She was interrupted from her deep thoughts by the children's screams and laughter as they exited the school. She noticed the kindergarten class walking in a perfect formation, as if they were little soldiers. The teacher directed Samantha to Jewels' car, and she got in.

"How was school, darling?"

"It was great, but I am ready to go home."

"Okie dookie, let's head home."

"Can we have spaghetti and meatballs for dinner?" asked Samantha.

"Spaghetti, it is, darling."

As they arrived home, Samantha rushed to the elevator to press the button.

Jewels opened the door to their apartment; she told Samantha to take off her school clothes and put on some comfy clothing. She could watch television or play on her tablet before dinner. As Jewels was unthawing the ground beef for the spaghetti, she heard a knock at the door.

She turned off the water and wiped her hands on a dish towel, heading toward the front door when a faint knock echoed through the apartment. Curious, she peeked through the peephole, her stomach tightened. William.

She froze. What the heck is he doing here?

For a moment, she debated ignoring it. But her hand was already on the lock. She cracked the door. "Why?" she asked flatly.

"Can I come in, please?"

Reluctantly, she opened it wider. "What are you doing here?"

William stepped inside, scanning the small apartment. "It's a nice little cozy place," he said, almost approvingly.

"Follow me into the kitchen," Jewels said, turning her back to him. She motioned for him to sit at the table while she went back to prepping dinner.

As he pulled out a chair, she glanced over her shoulder. "Alright, why are you here? And wait, how did you even know where I lived?"

A faint smile touched his lips. "You work for me, Jewels. I have ways of finding things out."

She gave him a look that was half disbelief, half annoyance. "Whatever. Just say what you came to say so you can leave."

He leaned forward, resting his arms on the table. "We need to talk."

"No, we don't," she shot back. "About what? We didn't have a relationship, William. We had lunch a few times, and then you asked to be one of my regulars….two or three days a week, like I was part of your schedule. That's not a relationship." She shook her head, her tone firm. "I left town to start a better life. There's nothing to talk about."

His jaw tightened. "It meant more to me than you think."

Jewels set the knife down on the cutting board and turned to face him fully. "Maybe it did for you. But for me? That life was killing me, William. I had to get out before I lost myself completely."

He searched her face, his voice dropping. "You didn't even say goodbye. One day you were there, the next… gone. You think I didn't care? You think I didn't wonder where you were, if you were okay?"

She swallowed hard but kept her gaze steady. "I'm not that woman anymore. And you… You're married now. We can't rewrite the past, and I'm not going back to it."

For a long moment, he didn't speak. Then he said quietly, almost like a plea, "I don't want to let you go again."

Jewel's eyes softened, but only for a second. "You already have, William. That part of my life is over."

She turned back to the counter, signaling the conversation was done. The scent of garlic filled the air, but the tension between them was thick, pressing in from every corner of the small kitchen. Jewel's jaw tightened as she sliced into a green pepper, the blade hitting the cutting board with a sharp rhythm.

Finally, she stopped mid-cut, the knife frozen in her hand. She turned, eyes blazing.

"First of all," she said, her voice low but burning, "you do not walk into my home and start asking me to go back to a lifestyle that no longer exists for me. And second…." her tone sharpened…. "there was never any great connection between us to rekindle. Not the way you're trying to make it sound. We shared moments, yes, but I left that life behind for a reason. So, with that said, you can leave."

She stepped toward him, gripping his arm to pull him up from the chair, but he jerked back, his eyes darkening.

Before either could say more, small footsteps pattered into the kitchen.

"Who is this, Mommy?" Samantha's voice was innocent, curious.

William looked down at her, his brow furrowing. There was something in her face, familiar in a way that made his chest tighten.

Jewels immediately pulled Samantha close to her side. "This is my daughter, Samantha."

William's gaze sharpened. "Is she the reason you left? Is she…."

"Stop," Jewels cut in, kneeling to meet Samantha's eyes. "Sweetheart, why don't you go play in your room? I'll come get you when dinner's ready."

"Okay!" Samantha chirped, already dashing off.

When she was gone, Jewels straightened. "No, William. She is not the reason I left."

He rose from the chair, closing the space between them in two strides. His hands came up, not touching her, but bracing against the counter on either side, keeping her there. "How old is she?" His voice was quieter now, but laced with an edge.

"She's five years old," Jewels said evenly.

William's expression shifted, suspicion blooming into something more personal. "Come on, Jewels. Why didn't you tell me?"

She blinked at him, stunned. "Tell you what?"

"That you were pregnant. That you had my child. Don't insult me by pretending it's a coincidence," he said, his voice low but steady, almost pleading.

Jewels stepped sideways, breaking his boxed-in stance, and motioned toward the table. "Please, sit down. I'll explain."

He hesitated but did as she asked, the legs of the chair were scraping against the tile.

Taking a breath, Jewels began. "Samantha isn't my biological daughter. I found her in a bathroom stall off the highway. She was two months old, abandoned in a car seat. There was no one else around. I couldn't just… leave her there. It hasn't been easy, raising her alone. But I had help, God's help and the community's. I adopted her officially through the court."

Her voice softened as she left the kitchen for a moment, returning with a small, folded note. "This was in her diaper bag the day I found her."

She handed it to him. William unfolded the paper slowly, reading the short, heartbreaking message. As his eyes scanned the words, his expression shifted from confusion to something more guarded, more troubled.

When he looked up at her again, his voice was tight. "I think… Samantha is my daughter."

# Chapter 17
## Paternity and Panic

Jewels closed the door slowly, her hand trembling on the knob. She stood motionless in the dim hallway, listening to the silence that followed William's departure. The thud of the door echoed in her ears, and her legs gave out beneath her. Sliding down the door, she collapsed onto the floor, pressing her forehead to her knees as tears spilled freely down her cheeks.

This can't be happening.

Her mind raced, struggling to process the shock of William's revelation. Samantha... his daughter? The words replayed over and over. She remembered the letter left in the diaper bag, the broken mother who had abandoned her child in a stall. How could she have known there was a connection to a man from her past?

Jewels wiped her face with the sleeve of her blouse and forced herself to breathe deeply. Amid her panic, one truth remained unshaken.... Samantha was hers. Maybe not by blood, but by bond, by love, by every bedtime story and scraped knee and first step. Jewels had chosen Samantha. She had fought for her and raised her. Loved her without condition.

She rose slowly, her legs still shaking. Peeking in on Samantha's room, she saw her curled under her pink unicorn comforter, fast asleep. Jewels leaned against the doorframe, overwhelmed by the sheer force of her maternal instinct. No one is taking her away from me.

She tiptoed back to the kitchen, grabbing the adoption paperwork from the drawer where she kept essential documents. She read every line, ensuring the adoption had been finalized legally and thoroughly. It had been five years. It was official. Samantha was hers. But still...

What if William challenged it?

Panic gripped her again. She needed advice. She needed someone she trusted.

She picked up her phone and called Malachi.

"Jewels?" his voice came groggy and concerned. "Everything alright?"

"Can you talk?" she whispered.

"Of course. What's going on?"

"I need to see you, first thing tomorrow morning. Please."

"Say no more. Meet me at the church. 8 AM."

"Thank you," she said, her voice cracking.

The next morning, Jewels dropped Samantha off at school like it was any other day. She kissed her forehead and gave her an extra-tight hug.

"Have a good day, sweetie."

"You too, Mommy!" Samantha chirped.

As she walked back to the car, the weight of the night returned with full force. She drove straight to the church, gripping the wheel tightly, her stomach in knots.

Malachi was waiting outside. He greeted her with a hug that melted some of her fear.

They sat in one of the side rooms, away from the bustle of volunteers and staff.

"I need help," Jewels said. "I don't know what to do."

She told him everything about William, the revelation, the letter, the abandoned baby, and the horrifying coincidence that Samantha might be his biological daughter.

Malachi listened without interrupting, his brows furrowed in concern.

"Do you have the adoption papers?"

Jewels handed them to him.

He scanned them thoroughly. "Everything looks airtight. You adopted her legally. You didn't lie. You didn't know."

"But what if he wants custody?"

Malachi leaned forward. "Jewels, listen to me. You've raised Samantha. You've loved her. You're her mother in every way that counts. And you have the law on your side. He would need a court order to challenge that adoption and from what you told me, even he was shocked."

Jewels nodded, but the fear still lingered.

"Then what do I do if he comes back?"

Malachi looked her in the eyes. "You stand your ground. You protect your daughter. And you get a lawyer, just in case."

That afternoon, Jewels picked Samantha up from school and tried to act normal. They went home, ate dinner, and watched cartoons together. She read to her, tucked her in, and kissed her goodnight like always.

But Jewels couldn't sleep.

She sat on the couch, laptop open, searching for family law attorneys in the city. She bookmarked a few, took notes, and then reached for the envelope where the original letter from the diaper bag had been tucked away. Her hands trembled as she reread it. "I can't do this. Please love her. Her name is Samantha."

It hurt to think about the mother who had felt so broken. It hurt more to think of Samantha being anyone else's responsibility.

Around midnight, her phone buzzed.

A text from William: "We need to talk again. Soon."

Jewels stared at the message, heart pounding.

She turned off the phone and went to her room. Lying in bed, she reached out and turned the light off.

She whispered into the darkness, "I didn't carry you in my womb, but I've carried you every day since. And I always will."

And with that, she finally drifted to sleep, knowing the fight wasn't over, but neither was her faith.

# Chapter 18
## Court Papers

"What is this?"

Jewels stared at the envelope on her desk, the courthouse seal glaring up at her. She unfolded the letter, her eyes scanning the words until the meaning hit like a slap. Petition for Custody. Filed by William Anderson.

What? Her heart pounded. What the heck is he doing? Two weeks ago, he promised he wouldn't pursue custody.

She stood abruptly, the letter crumpling slightly in her fist, and headed toward William's office. She forced herself to walk at a steady pace, not wanting to draw extra attention, even though every step made her want to storm in swinging a sledgehammer.

Remain calm. Find out why.

She knocked on his door.

"Come in," his voice called.

She entered, crossing the room and placing the paperwork squarely on his desk. "Why?"

A smirk tugged at his mouth. "Oh, I see you got the custody hearing paperwork."

"Yes," she said tightly. "What's this about?"

"After a long conversation with my wife," he began, leaning back in his chair, "we decided to seek custody of Samantha. It would be good for our family to have her live with us."

Her breath caught. Tears burned her eyes, blurring her vision. "Why are you doing this?"

He stood slowly, meeting her gaze without flinching. "Look, Jewels, she's my daughter, and I want custody. She should be with her blood relative..." His voice hardened. "...not a whore."

The words hit her like twenty-five hornets stinging all at once. Her knees buckled, and she caught herself on the back of a chair before she could fall.

She stood up straight and lifted her head. She looked into Williams' eyes and said, "You are not taking my daughter away from me." She turned around and walked out of the office.

As soon as she returned to her office, she called Mr. Wallace and told him about the custody paperwork she received from Samantha's biological father. She continued to say to him about their encounter five years ago.

Mr. Wallace told her to calm down, and he would file paperwork to establish paternity. Everything will be okay, Ms. Patton.

After the call ended, the words still echoed in her head, making it almost impossible to focus. Every email, every task at her desk felt mechanical, her mind somewhere else entirely. She got through the rest of the day on autopilot.

By the time she left work to pick up Samantha from school, her hands were trembling on the steering wheel, the weight of the news pressed against her chest like a stone.

When Samantha climbed into the back seat, she immediately noticed her mother's red, swollen eyes. Concern softened her small voice. "Is everything okay, Mommy?"

Jewels forced a smile, quickly swiping away the fresh tears that threatened to fall. "Yes, darling."

But Samantha was sharp, too observant for her age. "Then why are you crying?"

Jewel's throat tightened. "Don't worry, baby doll. Mommy just had a rough day at work."

Samantha tilted her head, her voice full of conviction. "Oh. Do you want me to send Tommy's father to your job?"

Jewels glanced at her in the rearview mirror, confused. "Tommy's father?"

"Yeah. He's a cop. He would go to your job and arrest the bad person who made you cry."

For the first time that day, Jewels let out a genuine laugh, the sound shaky but real. In that moment, she felt something crack open inside her…. not from pain, but from the fierce, pure love her daughter carried for her. It was a balm on her wounded spirit.

When they got home, the heaviness returned, but she had a little more strength to face it. She called Malachi, her voice quiet but steady, to ask if he could pick up Samantha from school on March 29. It was three weeks away.

He didn't hesitate. "Of course," he said, before asking gently, "Is something happening that day?"

Jewels swallowed hard. "It's the custody court hearing."

There was a pause, and then Malachi began to pray over the phone. His words like a warm shield, wrapping around her and pushing back the fear, if only for a moment. As she whispered "Amen," Jewels closed her eyes, holding onto the sound of his voice and the steady rhythm of Samantha playing in the other room, reminding her exactly what she was fighting for.

# Chapter 19
## The Battle Ends, but the War Within

Three weeks had passed, each one heavier than the last.

Jewels had done everything.... paperwork, attorney meetings, sleepless nights of prayer. But now, as the final custody hearing approached, her faith and strength were stretched to their limits.

William's betrayal echoed in her ears. "She's mine... she belongs with her blood, not a whore."

No. Jewels wouldn't let those words define her. She wasn't just fighting a legal case. She was fighting for Samantha, the little girl she chose in a bathroom stall and raised with nothing but grit, love, and the grace of God.

The morning of the hearing, Jewels sat on the edge of her bed, hands trembling as she tied her black heels. Samantha peeked in the door, clutching her teddy bear.

"You okay, Mommy?"

Jewels smiled, though her eyes were damp. "Yes, baby. Mommy has a big day today."

Samantha tiptoed over and kissed her mother on the cheek. "Don't be scared. God is with you."

Those simple words hit Jewels like a wind of peace. She wrapped her arms around Samantha, holding her for just a few seconds longer than usual.

At the courthouse, Jewels walked in beside Mr. Wallace, her attorney, head held high but heart pounding. She spotted William across the room, wearing an expensive navy suit, flanked by his lawyer. His eyes met hers for a moment and then darted away.

The judge entered, and everyone stood. The same judge from four years ago, who granted Jewels full custody then, now presided over what could unravel her entire world.

Opening statements were brief. Mr. Wallace laid out Jewels' case: years of consistent caregiving, emotional stability, and Samantha's thriving development. The opposing attorney focused on William's biological connection, financial capability, and claims that Samantha deserved a life of affluence.

When Jewels took the stand, her voice didn't waver.

"Your Honor, I may not share Samantha's blood, but I share every scraped knee, every bedtime story, every fevered night, and every early morning car ride to school. I chose her when no one else did. And I will choose her every day, for the rest of my life."

The courtroom was quiet.

William took the stand next. His voice was steady, but something in his eyes flickered with regret. Or calculation?

"I didn't know I had a daughter," he said. "Now that I do, I want her to be a part of my family. I can provide opportunities, stability... structure."

Jewels clenched her jaw. Structure meant nannies, cold meals, and shallow hugs.

As the judge reviewed the documents and testimonies, the silence in the room grew louder than any words spoken.

Then the gavel hit.

"After careful review of the evidence and in consideration of the best interest of the child, the court grants full custody to Jewels Patton. Mr. Anderson will receive limited visitation as scheduled by the court. This ruling is final."

Jewels exhaled, her hands shaking. Mr. Wallace smiled and whispered, "You did it."

But the peace was short-lived.

As she stood outside the courtroom, William brushed past, muttering, "Keep your charity project. I hope you enjoy raising someone else's problem."

Jewels stopped. She turned around, walked up to him, and said clearly, "She's not a problem. She's a purpose. And if you can't see that, then I'm even more thankful that the judge made the right choice."

She returned home that night exhausted. Samantha greeted her with open arms. Jewels bent down, picked her up, and held her tightly.

"Everything's okay now, baby. Mommy's not going anywhere."

Later that evening, after Samantha fell asleep, Jewels went to the kitchen table, opened her laptop, and began typing. Not for work, not for court, but for herself.

She began writing the story she'd lived, a testimony of faith, resilience, and the fight for love. The street work was behind her, but the street fight had just begun.

This time, she was fighting not just for survival, but for healing, wholeness, and a sense of purpose.

Chapter 19 ended not with a battle lost or won, but with a woman reclaiming her name, her motherhood, and her future.

And that woman's name was Jewels Patton.

# Chapter 20
## A New Beginning

Jewels stepped into the sunshine, exhaling deeply. Her spirit felt light for the first time in years.... maybe ever. For once, there were no court dates circled on her calendar, no looming threats, no lingering doubts. It was just her and Samantha now. Free.

She glanced back at the church. The sound of praise music drifted from inside, and the laughter of children echoed in the parking lot. It was the same church that had once embraced her when she was broken. And now, it wrapped her again in the warmth of new beginnings.

Samantha tugged at her hand, skipping along the pavement with joy. Jewels smiled.

"Mommy, can we get ice cream before we go home?"

"Of course," Jewels said. "Today we celebrate life."

She looked down at her daughter, her miracle and couldn't help but feel overwhelmed with gratitude. The past few weeks had been a whirlwind, but today felt like a breath of fresh air. Her little girl was safe, smiling, and unaware of the battles her mother had just fought and won.

As they walked toward their car, a man in a crisp navy suit stepped out of the side doors of the church, holding a tablet in one hand and a half-empty coffee in the other. His walk was deliberate, but there was a gentleness to his presence.

"Excuse me," he said. "Are you Jewels Patton?"

She turned slightly cautious. "Yes?"

"I'm Josiah Moore," he said, extending his hand with a warm but weathered smile. "Pastor Lacy said you've been volunteering a lot with the outreach program. I'm helping oversee the new family mentoring initiative."

Jewels shook his hand, sensing a strange familiarity in his voice. "Nice to meet you. I was telling Samantha it's time for ice cream."

Josiah glanced down and smiled at Samantha. "That's a very good reason to take a break. Can't beat ice cream on a sunny day."

Samantha giggled. "I'm getting strawberry!"

Jewels grinned and turned back to Josiah. "Are you new to the church?"

"Not exactly," he said. "Let's just say... I'm finding my way back." His eyes held a mix of grace and sorrow, like a man who had carried burdens too long without setting them down.

She nodded slowly. "Well, welcome back. Maybe we'll see you around."

"I hope so," Josiah replied, his voice calm and grounded.

Jewels watched him walk away toward a group of volunteers near the back of the building. Something about him lingered in her mind.... not attraction, not recognition, just a quiet curiosity. Maybe even a connection.

She retook Samantha's hand and headed for the car.

As they drove off, sunlight danced across the windshield, and the world felt wide open.

That evening, Jewels tucked Samantha into bed, pressing a gentle kiss to her forehead. "You're my greatest blessing," she whispered.

Samantha peeked one eye open. "I love you, Mommy. Forever."

Tears welled in Jewel's eyes as she quietly responded, "Forever and always."

Later, sitting at the kitchen table with a cup of tea, she opened her journal. The pages had long held her prayers, her confessions, and her rawest thoughts. Tonight, for the first time, her pen moved with peace instead of pain.

I am no longer who I was. And while the road here was broken and bruised, I'm stronger because of it. The storms didn't destroy me. They refined me.

She paused, thinking of Josiah. She didn't know his story yet, but she could see the storm behind his eyes, too. Maybe God was orchestrating something bigger. Perhaps their broken pieces would come together to form something whole.

Dear God, she wrote, *thank you for carrying me through. For Samantha. For second chances. For tomorrow.*

She closed the journal and whispered aloud, "It's a new beginning."

Outside, the wind rustled the leaves gently, as if Heaven was applauding her journey.

And maybe, just maybe, both of their stories were about to turn a new page together.

"When the Storm Alters Its Course"

*"Everyone has storms, but don't let the storms define who you are. We must continue to lean on God for hope, faith, and love. You will get through the storms."*

"He maketh the storm a calm, so that the waves thereof are still."
Psalm 107:29 KJV

*Book 2: Suffocating*

# Chapter 1
## A House Full of Light

Sunday morning sunlight streamed through the kitchen windows, catching the steam rising from Marsha's coffee cup. She was dressed in a navy skirt and cream blouse, her hair pinned neatly. Josiah stood at the counter, smoothing down Marcus's tie.

"You're choking me, Dad," Marcus grinned, adjusting his shirt collar.

"You'll live," Josiah teased, stepping back to inspect his work. "Looking sharp. Now grab your Holy scriptures, we're leaving in five."

They rode together in the family sedan, windows cracked just enough to let the spring breeze through. The smell of fresh-cut grass followed them to church, a red-brick building with white pillars and a steeple that could be seen three streets over. The parking lot was already filling with cars.

Inside, the sanctuary was alive with chatter, hugs, and handshakes. Elderly mothers in wide-brimmed hats fanned themselves with church programs, while children darted between the pews before their parents called them back. The choir was already warming up, their harmonies rolling through the room like sunlight on water.

Josiah and his family slid into their usual third-row pew, close enough to hear every word, far enough not to feel like they were on display.

When the opening hymns ended and announcements were given, Pastor Small stepped up to the pulpit, Holy scriptures in hand. He was a compact man in his late fifties, with a voice that could shift from velvet to thunder in a breath.

"Saints," he began, his tone rich and steady, "today we're going to talk about something that pleases God. And no, I'm not talking about singing in tune or putting a little extra in the offering plate. I'm talking about faith, the kind that moves mountains, breaks chains, and brings the impossible within reach."

He flipped his Holy scriptures open. "Hebrews 11:6 says: 'But without faith it is impossible to please him: for he that cometh to God must believe that he is, and that he is a rewarder of them that diligently seek him.'"

"Amen!" someone called from the back.

Pastor Small leaned forward, gripping the pulpit. "Without faith, church, it's not just difficult, it's impossible to please God. You can show up here every Sunday, know all the hymns by heart, and still miss His favor if you don't trust Him. Faith isn't just believing in God when the sun is shining, it's believing when the clouds roll in and the storm looks like it's here to stay."

Josiah felt the words press into him, not as a warning, but as a reminder. Life had been good lately steady work, a loving wife, a son who kept them laughing. Still, Josiah knew faith wasn't meant to be stored away for emergencies, it was a daily choice.

Pastor Small's voice softened. "To seek Him diligently means to chase after God like your life depends on it because it does. It means trusting His timing when yours is running out. It means saying, 'Lord, I don't see it yet, but I know You're working.'"

A murmur of agreement swept the room.

"And here's the promise," the pastor said, his hand lifting for emphasis. "When you believe… truly believe that He is who He says He is, He will reward you. Not always with what you want, but always with what you need to stand, to endure, to overcome."

Josiah's gaze drifted toward Marcus, who was following along in his Holy scriptures, underlining the verse. The boy's focus made him proud. Marcus had his mother's discipline and his father's steady hands, a combination Josiah knew would take him far.

By the time Pastor Small closed in prayer, Josiah's heart felt full. They stood for the benediction, voices joining together in one last hymn before filing out into the warm sunshine.

On the church steps, Marsha greeted friends while Marcus ran ahead to talk with his friends in the fellowship hall. Josiah lingered a moment, watching his family, his church, his community. Everything felt right.

As they drove home with the windows down, Marsha reached over and squeezed Josiah's hand.

"Good sermon today," she said.

He nodded. "Yeah. The kind you keep in your pocket for when life gets hard."

He didn't know just how much he'd need it someday. Their car pulled into the driveway.

When they stepped inside, the aroma of Marsha's slow-cooked roast and cornbread filled the house. "Table in twenty minutes," she called, slipping off her heels and tying on an apron.

Josiah loosened his tie, then leaned against the doorway to watch her work. "Woman, you're gonna have the whole neighborhood knocking if you keep cooking like this."

"That's fine," Marsha replied without looking up. "More mouths, more blessings."

Marcus set the table, lining up forks with meticulous precision. "Pastor Small was on fire today," he said. "Faith without doubting. That's what he meant, right?"

"That's it exactly," Josiah said, patting his son's shoulder. "Not just believing God exists but believing He is who He says He is. And then seeking Him, every day, every decision."

When the food was ready, they all bowed their heads. Josiah led the prayer, his voice low but steady. "Lord, thank You for this food, for our health, for our home. Thank You for the strength to work and the grace to rest. And thank you for my wife and my son, two of my greatest blessings. Amen."

They ate until the dishes were nearly bare. Marcus went back for seconds, then thirds. Marsha just shook her head. "This boy's got a bottomless pit for a stomach."

"Growing boy," Josiah said. "He'll be taller than me in no time."

After lunch, they moved to the living room. Sunlight spilled through the lace curtains, catching on the family photos that lined the mantel. Marcus sprawled on the rug, flipping through one of his science books. Marsha curled up in her chair with a magazine, and Josiah stretched out on the couch, hands behind his head.

"Daddy?" Marcus asked without looking up. "If God rewards those who diligently seek Him like Pastor said, does that mean He'll always give us what we pray for?"

Josiah thought for a moment. "Not always what we want, son. But always what we need. Sometimes His blessings look different from what we expect."

Marcus nodded slowly, returning to his book.

Outside, the late-afternoon breeze stirred the chimes on the porch, their soft notes mixing with the hum of the neighborhood. It was one of those rare, golden hours when everything felt still, whole, and unshakable.

Josiah didn't know, couldn't know that these were the moments he'd hold onto later when life would try to pull him under.

But for now, it was enough to be here. With them. In the blessing of an ordinary Sunday.

# Chapter 2
## Ordinary Wonders

Monday mornings in the Moore house moved like a practiced song. The scent of oatmeal and cinnamon drifted from the kitchen; the bathroom fan hummed; the dryer thumped a steady beat. Marsha worked the stove with one hand and scrolled through her calendar with the other, hair wrapped in a silk scarf, slippers whispering across tile.

"Marcus, five minutes," she called, sliding a pot off the burner. "Toast is popping in three... two..."

Pop. Pop.

"Incoming," Josiah said, catching the slices mid-air with a slight flourish and laying them on a plate. He wore his work chinos and a navy polo, still damp at the collar from the morning shave. He leaned toward his wife and bumped her shoulder. "You run this house like a command center."

Marsha smirked. "And you love it."

The hallway rattled and here came Marcus, seventeen and all limbs, socks mismatched, backpack half-zipped, a mechanical pencil tucked behind one ear.

"Mom, Dad.... good news." He held up a permission slip. "We're starting the cardio unit in biology today. We get to dissect a sheep heart next week."

Marsha made a face and set a bowl in front of him. "That's on your calendar. Do not bring anything home."

Josiah hid a smile and poured juice. "You can explain it to us, champ. Leave the organs at school."

"Deal." Marcus scooped oatmeal and blew across the spoon. "I'm building the capstone for the science fair, too. I was thinking a demo of a low-noise heart monitor, the kind I told you about, Dad. Remember? Something that still gives accurate readouts but doesn't sound like a horror movie in the ICU."

"That's my engineer," Josiah said. "What's your plan?"

"A microcontroller, pulse sensor, and a silicone baffle to dampen the speaker. I drew it out in my notebook. Please take me to McKenna Electronics after school. They have the exact sensor I want."

Marsha raised an eyebrow. "Budget?"

Marcus pressed his lips together. "I was hoping for... family sponsorship."

Josiah chuckled. "We'll see what parts cost after dinner. Earnest proposals get funded."

Marsha slid a napkin toward Marcus. "And earnest proposals wash their breakfast bowls."

He popped up, saluted, and ferried his dish to the sink. Moments later, they were out the door, Marsha with a lidded mug of tea, Josiah juggling keys and briefcase, Marcus with sneakers squeaking on the porch steps.

"Seatbelts," Marsha said automatically as they climbed in. "And Marcus? Don't speed through the hallways. Last week's near-collision with the tuba section gave me gray hairs."

"Noted," he said, grinning. "Love you, Mom. Love you, Dad."

"Love you," they answered, voices overlapping.

The day unfolded in its regular measures: emails and site checks for Josiah; appointment setting and patient filing at the doctor's office for Marsha; labs, essays, and cafeteria pizza for Marcus. By late afternoon, the family sedan swung by the school pick-up lane. Marcus jogged to the car, backpack bouncing.

"How was your day?" Josiah asked, easing into traffic.

"Sodium exploded in chemistry, so great." Marcus buckled in, then leaned forward. "McKenna's?"

"McKenna's," Josiah confirmed.

At the electronics shop, the bell above the door jingled. The place smelled faintly of solder and cardboard, Marcus's idea of perfume. Rows of bins labeled RESISTOR • CAPACITOR • SWITCH lined the walls like tidy treasure chests. Marcus moved among them with quiet reverence.

"Excuse me," he asked the clerk, "do you have the PulseWave P-100 sensor in stock? And a 10K variable resistor?"

"Two left," the clerk said, reaching below the counter. "You building a heart-rate kit?"

"A monitor that doesn't make kids cry," Marcus said, voice steady. "Hospitals can be scary. I want this to be… kind."

Josiah watched him, chest warm. It wasn't just that Marcus was brilliant; it was that he always bent smart toward good.

They left with a small bag of parts and a receipt that made Josiah wince only a little. In the car, Marcus rotated the sensor in his hand like it was a rare coin.

"Earnest proposal funded," Josiah said.

"I won't let you down," Marcus replied.

"You already don't."

At home, the kitchen became a shared workbench. Marsha chopped peppers and onions for fajitas. The sizzle from the skillet harmonized with the rhythmic click of Marcus's wire cutters at the table. He spread components over a clean dish towel; each piece neatly corralled: breadboard, jumper wires, microcontroller, pulse sensor coiled like a sleeping snail.

"Move your schematics off my placemats," Marsha said, leaning over to kiss the top of his head. "And put that soldering iron on a trivet."

"Yes, ma'am," he said, sliding everything an inch and a half.

Josiah joined them, forearms on the table, reading over Marcus's sketched plan. "You're routing signal to A0… good. And the baffle?"

Marcus lifted a small silicone ring. "I took one off an old phone case. I'm going to line the speaker with it to dampen the sound. See?" He pressed it to the tiny cone. "It's not perfect, but it'll lower the decibels."

"Prototype one," Josiah said. "We revise."

"Always," Marcus replied.

They ate together when dinner was ready, laughing about the day. Marsha shared a story about a group of seniors who learned to use video chat to connect with their grandkids at the doctor's office that she overheard from the waiting area. Josiah recounted a jobsite snafu that ended with a paint bucket and a shocked pair of loafers. Marcus, mouth full, offered to design a no-spill lid "with dignity."

"Blessing," Marsha said, spooning rice. "Blessing at every table."

"Blessing," the men echoed.

After dinner came clean-up, then project hour. Josiah pulled the desk lamp closer while Marcus attached the pulse sensor to his fingertip with a piece of medical tape. The screen blinked to life, numbers beginning to dance.

"It's reading," Marcus whispered, as if a louder voice might break the magic. "Look."

"Eighty-two BPM," Josiah read. "After fajitas? Seems fair."

"Speaker test," Marcus said, and toggled the baffle in place. The first chirp was sharp. He adjusted the silicone ring, then again. The next chirp softened, warm as rain on a roof.

Marsha drifted in with a mug of herbal tea. "That's gentler," she said. "If I were a patient, I wouldn't jump out of my skin."

Marcus sat back, pleased. "Good. That's the point."

They kept at it for another half-hour testing, tweaking, logging notes until Marsha tapped her watch. "Homework, shower, and lights at ten-thirty."

"Ten-fifteen," Josiah said, winking.

Marcus loaded his parts into a labeled box. "Fine, tyrants. But can I show you one more thing?" He held up a tiny 3D-printed clip. "It's a mount for kids' fingers, it'll make the sensor more comfortable. I'm going to ask the tech club to print a dozen."

Marsha smiled. "That's thoughtful, baby. Put it on your supply list, and I'll see what the office's printer can do."

"You're the best," he said, meaning it.

Later, while Marcus showered, Josiah and Marsha sat together on the couch, legs touching. The house exhaled after the bustle: dishwasher humming, porch chimes answering the wind.

"He's thriving," Marsha said softly. "I love the way his mind works."

"Me too." Josiah rubbed the back of his neck. "He asked for funding like a board presentation."

Marsha laughed. "He gets that from you. The meticulous part from me."

"And the heart from both of us," Josiah said.

Marsha leaned her head on his shoulder. "We're doing alright, Jo."

"We are," he said, and kissed her hairline.

When Marcus reappeared in pajama pants and an oversized camp T-shirt, he flopped into the chair opposite them, hair damp and curling at the edges.

"Mom, when can I drive on the highway?" he asked.

"When your guardian angels file for overtime and win," she said.

"Translation: Not yet," Josiah added. "We'll practice more in the neighborhood this week."

Marcus nodded, satisfied. He opened his notebook and scribbled a to-do list for the next day:

Print sensor clip (x12)

Code smoothing function

Ask Mr. Patel about resistor values

Bring Mrs. V. a spare charger (class tablet)

Marsha noticed the last line and smiled. "Always looking out for people."

He shrugged. "Feels right."

"Prayer before bed?" Josiah asked.

Marcus slid to his knees on the rug without a word. Marsha and Josiah joined him, forming a small triangle of hands and knees and quiet breath.

Josiah prayed first.... simple, steady. "Lord, thank You for today. For work we can do, food we can share, and peace in this house. Give us wisdom for every decision and joy for the ordinary things."

Marsha's voice followed, warm as a blanket. "Thank you for our son. Keep his mind sharp and his heart soft. Help us be the parents he needs."

Marcus cleared his throat. "Thanks, God. For parts that fit, code that runs, and... fajitas. Amen."

"Amen," his parents echoed, laughing.

They hugged in the hallway. Marsha kissed Marcus's cheek, and Josiah knocked twice on the doorframe—an old habit since Marcus was little.

"Night, champ," Josiah said.

"Night," Marcus replied, already half-turned toward his desk to line up tomorrow's supplies.

In their bedroom, Josiah set the alarm and slid beneath the covers. Marsha turned off the lamp, their room falling into a soft blue hum of streetlight and quiet house.

"This is my favorite kind of day," she whispered.

"The ordinary kind?" he asked.

"The blessed kind," she said.

He reached for her hand in the dark. "Faith makes it so," he murmured.

Down the hall, a desk lamp clicked off. In the living room, the dishwasher sang its end-of-cycle chime. The Moores slept under one roof, held by routine and love.... the steady, ordinary wonders that make a life.

Content Warning

The following chapter contains a fictional depiction of a school shooting.

It includes references to gun violence, emotional distress, and traumatic events that may be triggering or upsetting for some readers.

This content is presented with sensitivity and care to reflect the emotional impact on individuals and communities. Reader discretion is advised.

# Chapter 3
## The Wrong Person

"911, what's your emergency?"

"There's a school shooting at the local high school on the east side of town," Alisha whispered into her cell phone. "I'm hiding in the science room closet. Some kids are rampaging through the hallways and randomly shooting."

"How many gunmen are in the building?" the 911 operator asked, sounding like she was taking a delivery order.

"Two or three, I think. I didn't get a good look. I ran into an empty classroom on the second floor." The sound of footsteps coming down the hallway made her pause. "I hear someone coming. I have to go."

She pressed END and listened. In the hallway, a single pair of footsteps was approaching the classroom door. She closed her eyes and prayed: God, please don't let that door open!

A loud bang shook the room, and something hit the hallway door. She opened the closet door a crack and peeked, hoping she would see police officers. Instead, she saw Kevin Wood, who played football, standing in the doorway holding his right arm, which was bleeding profusely. She hurried over to the entrance and pulled him in.

"Are you hurt anywhere besides your arm?" Alisha whispered as loudly as she dared.

Kevin stared at her with glassy, unfocused eyes. He was going into shock.

As quickly as she could, Alisha looked him over for other wounds. Seeing none, she used her scarf as a tourniquet. It helped slow the bleeding, but the bullet must have hit a deep vein because she could not get it to stop. He needed to get to an emergency room fast.

She heard multiple emergency vehicles entering the school grounds as she continued to apply pressure on Kevin's arm. Faintly, Kevin said, "Thank you."

"Don't thank me yet, help is on the way," she replied. Alisha crawled to the open window to signal for help. She found a piece of paper and a marker, wrote the words "HELP ME" on it, and then held it out of the window.

She banged on the window to gain the attention of all the officers entering the building. She noticed one of them looking up and saw her sign. He signaled for two officers to head to the second floor of the building.

On the other side of the school building, two of the gunmen were apprehended, while one of the gunmen was still hiding in the school. While Marcus was running, he turned the corner. The fire alarm blared in shrill, chaotic pulses. Lockdown lights flashed red. The school had turned into a maze of panic and confusion, students screaming, doors slamming, and feet thundering down the halls. Marcus ran, heart pounding, lungs burning, trying to make it to the nearest exit. He had been in the gym when the chaos started. No weapon. No threat. Just the instinct to survive.

As he rounded the corner near the science wing, he stopped dead in his tracks.

Officer Johnson.

Gun drawn.

"Freeze!" Johnson shouted, his voice sharp and guttural, slicing through the noise like a blade.

Marcus raised his hands instinctively, breath catching in his throat. "I-I'm not the one," he stammered. "I'm not... please...."

But Johnson had already moved, wide stance, eyes narrowed. His hand gripped the pistol so tightly his knuckles went white. Sweat rolled down his temple. The radio on his shoulder crackled: "Shooter last seen in a dark hoodie, male, possibly armed, headed toward west hall."

Marcus wore a dark hoodie.

"No sudden moves!" Johnson barked. "Get on the ground! Now!"

"I'm not him!" Marcus gasped. "I was running from the gunshots…. I swear, I was just trying to get out!"

But Johnson didn't hear the words. Or maybe he did, but they couldn't pierce the years of conditioning, the muscle memory, the fear. All he saw was a figure in a hoodie running through a school during a shooting.

Just like the reports said.

Marcus's hands trembled in the air. "Look at me! I don't have anything! Check my bag! I'm just trying to get home…"

But the world slowed.

Johnson's finger twitched.

The shot rang out.

Marcus staggered backward like the sound itself had struck him first then came the impact, a hot, searing punch to his chest. His legs gave way beneath him, and he crumpled to the tile floor, gasping, eyes wide in disbelief, blood blooming beneath him like a red halo.

"I…." he tried to say something else, but the words drowned in blood and silence.

Johnson stood frozen, gun still raised, face drained of color as reality crashed down on him like a tidal wave.

Marcus wasn't the shooter.

He was a kid.

A boy running for safety.

And he would never finish his sentence.

Keith and Alex, who were running behind him, quickly ran to Marcus' aid to help, but it was too late. They thought that it was the other gunman who had shot him, but as they looked up, it was a police officer.

"Oh my God, he's not the gunman," Officer Johnson said.

"No," said the boys.

"We were trying to escape from the back entrance, we were hiding in the gym bleachers, and now you killed a hostage," replied Alex.

The officer was terrified of shooting and killing a student during a school shooting. He was unsure of how to tell his commanding officer.

Officer Johnson radioed Lt. Miller to request that EMS come to the back entrance as soon as possible. Within three minutes, another officer radioed about apprehending the last suspect.

His heart dropped to the floor, and he threw up. The boys looked at each other and felt bad. Officer Johnson was pacing the floor, mumbling and holding his chest.

As the boys were sitting next to Marcus' motionless body, they saw the EMS team running with a gurney.

"Move back, boys," said one of the EMS staff members as they entered to reach the scene.

They tried to revive Marcus, but it was too late. "What happened?" said the EMS staff member.

Before the children could answer, Officer Johnson said, "The boys were running the gym with a student who had been shot by one of the gunmen, but it was too late to save him. They weren't able to make it out of the school before he collapsed in their arms."

Alex and Keith exchanged a glance with wide eyes as the officer lied. More officers rushed in and escorted the boys out of the school.

Alex whispered, "We have to tell the truth; that guy just lied."

"I know, I'm telling my mom when she arrives," replied Keith.

"Me, too."

As the gunmen were arrested and transported to the police station, all students waited outside in the parking lot for their parents to arrive.

# Chapter 4
## The World Stops

The television screen in the break room flickered as the regular daytime news was interrupted.

"Breaking News: Reports of an active shooter situation at the local high school. Law enforcement and first responders are currently on the scene. Parents are being urged to avoid the area until further notice."

Josiah dropped the pen in his hand. His heart stuttered at the local high school. That was Marcus's school.

"Josiah," a coworker whispered, eyes still glued to the screen, "Isn't that where your boy goes?"

He didn't answer. He was already running.

Across town, Marsha stood frozen behind her desk at the medical clinic. She had been prepping patient files when the news broke. Her fingers trembled as she picked up her phone. No messages. No texts. No call from Marcus.

She dialed his number, but it went straight to voicemail.

Her legs buckled as she grabbed her purse and bolted out the door, shouting over her shoulder, "Family emergency.... I'm gone!"

The parking lot outside of the school was a storm of screaming, sobbing, sirens, and frantic movement. Children.... some barefoot, some still in blood-splattered gym clothes.... cried out for their parents. Others stood frozen, clinging to one another like lifelines. The air was sharp with the scent of smoke and adrenaline.

Parents slammed their car doors and ran full speed toward the barricade line, some yelling names, others pushing past officers to see a glimpse of their child. Emergency lights painted the scene in red and blue waves, blinking against terrified faces.

Josiah skidded into the lot, eyes wild. "Marcus!" he shouted, voice cracking. "Marcus Moore!"

"Sir, you need to stay behind the line!" an officer yelled.

But Josiah wasn't listening. His eyes scanned every child's face, praying begging to find his.

"No. No…. I don't see him." Josiah's hands gripped his head, eyes scanning the chaos like a man trying to read in a storm. "I called…. nothing. I called again, voicemail."

"Where is my baby?" Marsha's voice broke, the words splintering in her throat. Her eyes darted everywhere searching every cluster of people, every uniform. Her pulse pounded so loudly she could barely hear the sirens screaming around them.

The parking lot was a mess. Children sobbed in their parents' arms. Teachers shouted names over the blare of radios. Police moved people away from the barricades. Somewhere, a news crew was setting up a camera, the reporter's hair whipped by the wind. The air was cold, carrying the metallic tang of exhaust and the faint chemical bite of gunpowder that still clung to someone's clothes.

A boy stumbled past, his backpack hanging open, tears carving tracks down his cheeks before he collided with his mother's arms. Marsha froze, her chest twisting. Every reunion stabbed. Each hug she saw was one she didn't get.

"Marcus!" Josiah shouted, his voice cracking but loud enough to cut across the noise. "Marcus!"

Nothing.

They pushed through the crowd, weaving between clumps of sobbing families and officers with guarded expressions. The smell of coffee from a half-crushed paper cup on the ground mixed with the sharp scent of cold air.

Then Josiah spotted him, a uniform with brass on the collar, the posture of someone who knew more than he could say. Josiah grabbed Marsha's hand, pulling her toward him.

"Lieutenant!" Josiah's voice carried urgency. "We can't find our son. Marcus Moore. He's not with the evacuated students…. no one's telling us anything!"

The Lieutenant looked at them, his jaw tightening before softening a fraction. "Sir, ma'am, this isn't the place for that conversation. Please come with me. The Chief has asked to speak with you directly."

Marsha's breath stuttered. "Please.... just tell me..."

"Not here," the Lieutenant said firmly, lowering his voice. "It's urgent. Follow me."

They exchanged a terrified glance, then followed him to a patrol car. The door closed, sealing out the wind and the shouting, leaving only the hum of the engine and the heavy sound of their breathing. In the rearview mirror, the school shrank away, lights flashing, chaos receding until all that remained was dread.

When they arrived at the police station, they were escorted through a side entrance, away from cameras, down a quiet hallway that smelled faintly of old coffee and cleaning supplies.

The conference room was dim, blinds drawn against the late afternoon sun. The air felt still, almost too still. A pitcher of water and two glasses sat in the center of the table, untouched.

Chief Nelson and Commissioner Anderson stood as they entered. "Mr. and Mrs. Moore," Nelson said softly. "Please... sit."

Marsha sat on the edge of her chair, hands clasped so tightly her knuckles were bloodless. Josiah sat stiffly, both feet planted as if bracing for a hit.

Nelson leaned forward, elbows on the table. "I'm sorry we have to meet under these circumstances. There was a lockdown at the school today. During that time, one of our officers encountered your son in a hallway. Based on the information coming in at the time, he matched the description of the suspect of a male, dark hoodie, running."

Josiah's voice was tight, the words scraped raw. "And what happened next?"

Nelson hesitated just long enough for the air to grow heavy. "The officer discharged his weapon. Your son was struck. He was transported immediately, but…" He swallowed, voice faltering for a beat. "…he did not survive."

Marsha's hands flew to her mouth. A choked, animal sounds like escaped from her mouth as she bent forward, shoulders shaking.

Josiah's voice cracked, rising with fury. "You want to pacify us with procedures? My son was seventeen. He wanted to be a doctor. He wore that hoodie because it was cold outside, not because he was dangerous!"

Marsha stood abruptly, trembling but fiercely. "Do you know what it's like to bury your child because someone trained to protect them pulled a trigger instead? Do you know what it's like to sit in your living room and see your son's face on the news under the word victim? Not suspect. Not a threat. Victim. And all we get is 'we're looking into it'?"

"I promise you," Nelson said carefully, "we are taking this seriously. There will be transparency. There will be accountability."

Josiah gave a sharp, bitter laugh. "You want to talk about accountability now? You let a man walk out of that building today who ended a child's life with one bullet and one assumption."

Nelson's gaze dropped. "I underst-"

"No, you don't understand," Josiah said flatly. "You get to go home tonight. You get to hug your child. I get to pick out a casket."

The room went silent except for the faint ticking of a wall clock. Marsha's sobs were quieter now but deeper, like something breaking apart inside her.

Nelson finally cleared his throat. "I know this is unbearable. But we need you to identify Marcus's body at the coroner's office. Officer Green will escort you."

Marsha turned her face away. Josiah stood slowly, his shoulders squared but his eyes got wet. He didn't speak, he just nodded once.

A young officer stepped into the doorway, her face pale. "I'll take good care of them, sir," she said quietly.

Josiah and Marsha followed her out, their footsteps sounding heavy and final in the quiet hallway.

Behind a locked door, Officer Johnson sat slumped in a chair, his badge on the table like a weight he could no longer carry. His shirt was unbuttoned at the collar, his hands buried in his hair.

Nelson and Anderson entered without a word.

"You never gave him time to explain," Nelson said, his voice tight. "You didn't wait for backup. You didn't verify. You acted. And now a boy with dreams is gone."

Tears slid down Johnson's face. "I see his face every time I blink," he whispered. "I see his hands in the air."

"You're being placed on administrative leave effective immediately," Anderson said. "Turn in your service weapon. Your access is revoked until further notice. There will be a full investigation, and you will cooperate fully."

Johnson nodded numbly.

"And listen carefully," Nelson added. "No statements. No interviews. Stay away from the school. Stay away from the family. Let this investigation take its course."

Johnson slowly set his gun beside his badge. "I didn't mean to kill him," he said, voice breaking.

Nelson's expression was grave. "Intent doesn't undo impact."

They stepped out, leaving Johnson alone. The silence in the room pressed in until it felt suffocating. And in that silence, Officer Johnson wept—not just for Marcus, but for the line he had crossed and the life he could never return.

The ride over to the Coroner's office was wordless. Josiah stared out the window, hands locked together until the skin over his knuckles stretched white. Marsha's grip on his arm was unrelenting. Officer Green kept her eyes on the road, the hum of the tires the only sound.

The hallway to the viewing room was long, sterile, and suffocatingly quiet. Every step felt like dragging cement blocks through a nightmare.

They stopped in front of a steel door. Officer Green keyed in a code, her voice hushed. "Take your time. He's inside."

The lock clicked. Josiah and Marsha stepped in together.

The lights were dim. The air was still. The white-tiled walls were indifferent to the grief they contained. On the table beneath a thin white sheet lay what had once been life…. dreams, laughter, heartbeat, future. Now only stillness.

Marsha broke first. "No…" she whispered, then louder, "No, no, no, no…"

She stumbled forward, dropping to her knees beside the table, sobbing so hard her shoulders shook. She whispered Marcus's name over and over, as if saying it could pull him back. The coroner pulled the thin white sheet back.

Josiah stood frozen.

There he was.

Marcus Elijah Moore.

His face was calm, unnaturally calm, his eyes gently closed as if he'd fallen asleep mid-dream. A bruise darkened his chest near the stitched bullet wound.

Josiah's knees nearly buckled. He gripped the table edge to stay upright. "I told him to wear the hoodie…" His voice was barely audible. "It was cold outside. I told him…"

Marsha's wails ricocheted off the cold tile, jagged and unrestrained, filling the sterile room with a grief that had no boundaries. Josiah stood frozen, his breath caught somewhere between his chest and his throat, the sound of her cries tearing at him in places he didn't know could hurt.

His vision blurred, not from tears alone, but from the crushing weight pressing in on every side. The walls seemed to close in. The air was too thick. The fluorescent light above hummed, oblivious to the shattering of two hearts.

Marsha clung to their son's still body, rocking as if she could breathe life back into him. "My baby… my baby…" she repeated, the words collapsing under their own weight. Josiah's hands trembled as he reached out, not sure whether he was trying to steady her or himself.

He wanted to scream. To bargain. To wake up. But all that came was silence thick, suffocating silence, broken only by the sound of her sobs echoing in a room that would never hear their son's laughter again.

# Chapter 5
## The House That Holds the Silence

The ride home from the coroner's office felt longer than the drive there. Neither of them spoke. Josiah kept his eyes on the road, hands locked around the steering wheel like letting go would send him into a freefall. Marsha stared out the passenger window, her reflection in the glass looking older than she had had the day before.

When they pulled into the driveway, the world looked wrong.

The sun was still shining. A neighbor across the street was raking leaves. Somewhere, a dog barked.

But on their porch, Marcus's backpack still hung from the hook, right where he had dropped it the day before.

Josiah opened the door, and the silence hit them like a wall.

The air was still. The house smelled faintly of cinnamon from the candle Marsha had lit that morning. Every room seemed to hold echoes, Marcus laughing as he ran down the hall, the thud of his sneakers on the stairs, the time he burned toast in the kitchen and tried to cover it with cologne so no one would smell it.

Now, all of it was gone.

Not the objects, not the air, but the life in it.

Josiah hung up his coat but didn't move farther into the house. Marsha walked past him, her steps slow, pausing at the bottom of the stairs like she was thinking of going up then turning away.

The knock on the door came before they could sit down.

Marsha's sister, Lorraine, stood there with her husband and two teenage sons. Behind them were three of Marsha's closest friends from church, each holding foil-covered casserole dishes.

The entryway filled quickly with the sound of low voices and the smell of food.

"Sweetheart…" Lorraine wrapped Marsha in a long, warm hug. Marsha didn't cry then, but her grip was fierce, like she was afraid letting go would make her fall apart.

The friends stayed for a while, offering scripture, holding her hands, praying over them both. Josiah sat in the armchair, nodding when spoken to, but his mind floated somewhere else. He caught pieces of verses "The Lord is close to the brokenhearted..." but they felt like they were coming from underwater.

After they left, more visitors came. A neighbor brought bread. Someone from the church dropped off flowers. A deacon offered to help with funeral arrangements. Josiah thanked each one, shook hands, and promised to call if they needed anything.

By nightfall, the house was full of food but empty of sound.

Marsha sat on the couch with a blanket around her shoulders, staring at a plate she hadn't touched. Josiah stood at the window, watching the last streak of light fade.

When she finally spoke, her voice was quiet. "How do we even do this?"

Josiah turned toward her. "One day at a time."

She shook her head slowly. "One breath at a time."

Later, when Marsha went upstairs, Josiah stayed in the living room. He opened the worn Holy scriptures that had belonged to his father and found himself in the book of Job.

His eyes blurred as he read: "The LORD gave, and the LORD hath taken away; blessed be the name of the LORD."

The words sat heavy in his chest. He didn't understand. He didn't have answers. But he found himself whispering anyway:

"Lord... through my pain and sorrow... I will not turn from You."

He continued to sit in the living room long after the candle went out, the Holy scriptures still open in his lap. Somewhere upstairs, Marsha's footsteps moved softly across the bedroom floor, then stopped.

The quiet pressed in until it felt almost too heavy to breathe.

Finally, Josiah stood. His body moved on its own, carrying him down the hall and up the stairs. His hand hesitated on the doorknob of Marcus's room.

When he opened it, the air was thick with his son's scent, laundry detergent, the faint musk of teenage cologne, and something warmer, something only a parent could recognize. He looked around the room.

The desk was cluttered with notebooks and sketches. A science textbook lay open, a pencil still marking the last problem he'd worked on. The bed was unmade, the blanket twisted like he'd just climbed out of it that morning.

Josiah stepped inside slowly, fingers brushing across the edge of the desk. He noticed a crumpled paper sat near the lamp, Marcus's handwriting in blue ink:

"Become Dr. Marcus Moore, help people heal."

Josiah's throat tightened until it hurt to swallow. He sat on the edge of the bed, gripping the paper in both hands, the edges soft from his fingers pressing too hard.

"God…" His voice was barely a whisper. "How do I walk through a world that still turns without him?"

He didn't expect an answer. But in the stillness, he felt the same quiet presence that had been with him in the coroner's office.

It didn't erase the ache. It didn't make the tears stop.

But it told him he was not alone.

Josiah laid the paper back near the lamp exactly where he'd found it, then turned out the light and left the door slightly open just the way Marcus always did when he slept.

# Chapter 6
## Saying Goodbye

The morning air felt colder than it should have been for early spring. Josiah sat on the front porch, his navy-blue suit pressed, white bow tie neat, Marcus's favorite color combination. His hands rested on his knees, still as stone.

When the family car pulled up, he stood. The driver stepped out to open the door. Inside, Marsha sat between her parents, her eyes hidden behind dark sunglasses. Her mother looked him over.

"Why not black?" she asked flatly.

Josiah kept his voice even. "This is a homegoing. My son's favorite color was navy blue. I'm wearing it to honor him."

She said nothing else, but her disapproval hung in the air like fog. Marsha didn't speak, just looked out the window as they pulled away.

The funeral home parking lot overflowed with cars. Clusters of students in black suits and dresses huddled together, their voices low. Teachers stood near the entrance. News cameras lingered at the edges, their lenses waiting like vultures.

Inside, the air smelled faintly of lilies and wood polish. A massive collage of Marcus's photos stood near the front, him on his dirt bike, bent over his science textbooks, laughing with friends.

Marsha's breath hitched when she saw it. Josiah reached for her hand. She let him take it, but her fingers stayed stiff in his grip.

They sat in the front row, family on either side. The soft hum of the organ filled the silence. Muffled sobs echoed from somewhere behind them.

When the service began, speakers rose one by one. Teachers spoke of Marcus's curiosity. Friends remembered his kindness. Josiah's turn came, and he gripped the podium, the wood warm under his palms.

"My son wanted to be a doctor," he began. "Not because it was a good career, but because he wanted to heal people. That was who he was, a healer, even at seventeen. He believed that one person could make a difference... and he proved it every day he lived."

His voice trembled only once, when he said Marcus's name.

Marsha followed, her hands shaking as she held the microphone. "Marcus had a laugh that filled a room. He asked questions no one else thought to ask. He was the best thing that ever happened to me in my life. And I will miss him... until my last breath."

Her voice cracked, but she finished, placing the mic back in its stand before quickly returning to her seat. She didn't look at Josiah.

At the gravesite, the sky had darkened, clouds pressing low. The pastor's voice carried over the wind. "Earth to earth, ashes to ashes, dust to dust..."

The casket lowered slowly, the ropes creaking under its weight. Marsha's shoulders shook beside him. Josiah's chest tightened so much he thought he might not be able to breathe.

He reached for her hand again. This time, she didn't take it.

"You were everything to us," Marsha whispered toward the open sky, her voice trembling.

The pastor prayed. Mourners laid single white roses on the casket. One by one, the crowd began to drift away.

Josiah stayed.

Even after the last car pulled away, he stood at the edge of the grave, the cold wind tugging at his suit. He didn't cry. He didn't move. He just stared at the rectangle of earth that had swallowed his only child.

When the groundskeeper finally approached, Josiah gave a slight nod and turned toward the road. He walked home alone.

The house met him in silence.

He stood in the doorway for a long time before stepping inside, the scent of lilies from the funeral clinging to his clothes. Marsha's shoes were gone from their usual spot by the door. Her coat was missing from the hook.

He didn't call out for her.

Instead, Josiah hung up his jacket, loosened his bow tie, and sank into the chair in the corner of the living room.

The silence of the house was heavier than the graveyard.

The morning after the funeral, Josiah woke to the kind of silence that he felt alive.

Not peaceful. Not empty. Alive.

Every creak of the old floorboards, every faint hum of the refrigerator, every sigh of the wind against the windows seemed to carry the memory of what it had been.

Marsha was already up. The faint sound of clinking dishes came from the kitchen, but there was no smell of breakfast. No scent of coffee. Just the motion of someone avoiding stillness.

Josiah sat on the edge of the bed for a long time before finally standing. He showered, dressed in a plain gray sweatshirt, and wandered into the kitchen.

Marsha stood at the sink, staring out the window. Her hands rested on the counter, motionless.

"Morning," he said quietly.

She didn't look at him. "Your mother called yesterday."

"My mother's gone," Josiah said.

"I mean your aunt," she corrected quickly. "She wanted to check in."

Josiah nodded. "I'll call her later."

They spoke like that all morning, clipped sentences, neutral voices, as if any emotion would break something fragile between them.

The day passed in slow motion. A few people called a deacon from church, a detective from the department who "just wanted to touch base." None of the conversations gave him anything to hold onto.

In the afternoon, Josiah found himself standing at Marcus's door. His hand hovered over the knob before he finally turned it.

The air inside smelled like laundry detergent and the faint, sharp tang of the body spray Marcus used after basketball practice. The desk was cluttered with notebooks and open textbooks, pages filled with neat handwriting. On the nightstand sat a model heart, half-finished, its tiny plastic arteries and veins waiting to be snapped into place.

Josiah sat on the bed, his hands pressed to his knees. He stared at the model heart until his vision blurred.

On the floor by the bed was a piece of paper folded, worn at the edges. He picked it up. Inside, in Marcus's handwriting, were the words:

"Don't quit. Ever. Love you, Dad."

Josiah pressed the paper to his forehead and closed his eyes. His breath came slowly and unevenly.

That evening, Marsha's sister dropped by with a casserole. She stayed in the kitchen with Marsha, their hushed voices carrying just far enough for Josiah to know they were talking about him. He didn't ask what was said.

When the house was quiet again, he sat at the kitchen table with his father's old Holy scriptures. His hands opened it without thinking, and his eyes fell on Job 2:10:

"Shall we receive good at the hand of God, and shall we not receive evil?"

He let the words sit there. They didn't erase the ache. They didn't make sense of it. But they were true.

Josiah whispered into the stillness, "Lord... I don't understand this. But I'm still Yours."

The quiet didn't answer. But it didn't feel empty anymore.

# Chapter 7
## Cracks in the Foundation

Three days had passed since the funeral.

The fridge was packed with untouched food from neighbors and friends. The flowers from the service sat on the counter, their petals already curling at the edges. The house smelled faintly of lilies, coffee, and something else Josiah couldn't name, the scent of a place that had lost its center.

Marsha was in the living room when Josiah came down the stairs that morning. She sat on the couch, her laptop open, a half-drunk cup of tea beside her.

"What's that?" Josiah asked.

"An email from a legal aid group," she said without looking up. "They handle wrongful death cases. One of my friends from church sent it to me."

Josiah pulled out a chair at the kitchen table. "Marsha…"

She closed the laptop and turned toward him, her eyes already tired. "We can't just sit here. We need to be talking to lawyers, to the press, to anyone who will make sure Marcus's name isn't forgotten."

"We're not forgetting him," Josiah said quietly. "But running out there, shouting before the investigation is even done… it won't change what happened."

Her voice sharpened. "So, we just do nothing?"

"We pray. We wait. We let the truth come out."

Marsha's hands clenched in her lap. "Prayer doesn't make people listen, Josiah. Action does. And right now, it looks like you don't care."

His jaw tightened. "Don't say that. I care more than you can imagine. I believe God's justice is stronger than mine."

She shook her head slowly. "That sounds like an excuse."

The day passed in separate rooms.

Marsha made phone calls from the living room, her voice low but urgent. Josiah worked in the office, though he barely touched the papers in front of him. The air between them felt like a stretched cord, one wrong word and it would snap.

That evening, they ended up in the kitchen at the same time. She was making tea; he was pouring water into a glass.

"Are you coming to the vigil on Saturday?" she asked.

"I hadn't decided," he said.

"You hadn't decided?" She turned toward him fully now. "They're lighting candles for our son, and you can't decide if you want to be there?"

Josiah took a breath, slow and steady. "I don't want to stand in front of cameras while people take pictures of my grief like it's a news story. That's not how I want to honor him."

Marsha stared at him for a long moment, then set her mug down hard enough to splash tea over the rim. "Maybe I don't even know who you are anymore."

She left the kitchen without another word.

Later that night, Josiah heard her on the phone in their bedroom. Her voice was hushed, but the words carried just enough for him to know she was talking to her mother. He heard his name once, then silence.

He stayed on the couch until she turned out the light upstairs.

Lying there in the dark, he prayed again not for answers, not for justice, but for strength.

Because he could feel the next wave coming, and he knew it would take everything in him not to drown.

# Chapter 8
## The Breaking Point

The morning was gray, the kind that made the air feel heavy. Josiah woke to the sound of drawers opening and closing upstairs. At first, he thought Marsha was tidying, but then he heard the unmistakable sound of a zipper.

When he came into the bedroom, she was kneeling beside the bed, folding clothes into a suitcase.

"What are you doing?" His voice was low, but it carried.

She didn't look up. "I'm going to stay at my mother's for a while."

Josiah stepped closer. "A while? Or for good?"

She paused, her hands still on the fabric. "I don't know yet."

"Marsha…" His throat tightened. "We've barely had time to breathe. Why now?"

She sat back on her heels, finally meeting his eyes. "Because I can't breathe here, Josiah. Every corner of this house reminds me of him, and every time I look at you, I see someone who refuses to fight."

"I'm fighting in my way," he said.

She shook her head. "Your way is quiet. Too quiet. And I can't live in it anymore."

He felt the floor tilt beneath him. "So, you're just leaving?"

"I'm selling the house," she said flatly. "We can't keep it. It's too much… for both of us."

His voice sharpened. "This is our home."

"It was our home," she corrected softly. "But without him, it's just walls."

She zipped the suitcase, stood, and brushed past him. He didn't follow her downstairs. The sound of the front door closing echoed through the house like a slammed book.

Josiah stood in the hallway for a long time, staring at nothing. When he finally moved, it was toward the kitchen. He opened a cabinet and saw it, a half-full bottle of strong liquor from before Marcus died.

He took it down. His hands felt heavier just holding it.

On the counter, he set out a glass and poured a shot. The clear liquid caught the gray light from the window.

He lifted it halfway to his lips, then stopped. He inhaled a sharp, chemical, wrong. He looked at the glass again, then at his reflection in the kitchen window.

"I can't," he muttered.

The words came out stronger the second time. "I can't."

He turned and dumped the vodka into the sink. The smell filled the air for a moment before disappearing down the drain.

Josiah gripped the counter, his head bowed. "Lord... don't let me fall apart like this. Show me another way to stand."

The tears came hard then unplanned, unstoppable. He slid down to the floor, curling his knees to his chest, his body rocking gently like a child.

The house creaked around him, empty and too large. The only sound left was the quiet, steady rhythm of his own breathing, the proof that, despite it all, he was still here.

# Chapter 9
## The Shuttered Doors

The weeks after Marsha left were long and colorless.

Josiah kept busy or at least he tried. Work was all he had left, and TrueBeam Build Co. had been his pride for fifteen years. The office felt quieter without Marcus dropping by after school to tinker with tools or sneak a soda from the break room fridge.

He thought throwing himself into the business would keep his mind from spiraling. But little cracks began to show almost immediately.

A supplier called one morning about a late payment.

Then another.

By the third call in a week, Josiah started digging into the company's books himself.

It was a Thursday when he found them.

Two large deposits each from a client he didn't recognize followed by even larger withdrawals made out to "cash." The total loss? Over $260,000. Not enough to cover payroll and materials for several major contracts.

His chest tightened. He double-checked the client names. Nothing. No contracts. No job numbers. No invoices.

Josiah called George into his office, sliding the printed statements across the desk.

"Who processed these?"

George frowned. "I didn't. Jerry handled the downtown jobs while you were out."

Josiah's voice hardened. "These aren't jobs. They're fake."

Jerry hadn't been in the office for over a week. When Josiah and George drove to his apartment, an elderly neighbor opened the door.

"He packed up fast," she said. "Said he came into some money and was moving out of state. Didn't say where."

Josiah thanked her, but his stomach sank. "Came into money" could only mean one thing.

The bank confirmed his fears the account was frozen pending investigation. It could take months to recover any funds, if they recovered them at all. Payroll was due in five days. A supplier threatened to pull materials from two job sites. The new marketing campaign, the product line all of it stalled overnight.

Josiah filed a police report the same day. Detective Luke Mitchell listened, flipping through the file of statements and transaction screenshots Josiah had prepared.

"This is substantial," Mitchell said. "We'll pursue criminal charges, but I can't promise how quickly we'll track him down."

Josiah nodded, though the words felt like air. "I just need to keep my company alive."

He tried everything.

Meetings with the bank. Calls to potential investors. Applying for an emergency line of credit and selling off unused equipment.

Every door closed in his face.

One night, sitting in the empty office long after dark, Josiah stared at the numbers on the balance sheet until they blurred. His credit cards were maxed. His savings were gone. The contracts he'd worked years to build were slipping away.

When the final loan denial came through, he sat back in his chair and let the weight of it hit him.

He thought of Marcus. He thought of Marsha. And now this, the one thing he had left was being stripped away.

The next morning, he filed the paperwork to dissolve TrueBeam Build Co.

That afternoon, Josiah walked through the office one last time. The desks were empty, the break room quiet. The sign out front still bore the company's name, but the keys in his hand suddenly felt like they belonged to someone else.

He locked the door and stood on the sidewalk, staring at the building.

"Fifteen years," he murmured. "And it's gone."

In the stillness, he prayed not loudly, not with eloquence, but with the raw honesty of a man standing in the ruins of his life.

"Lord... I don't understand why you're taking everything. But I won't turn away."

The wind carried no answer. But Josiah turned the keys in, walked to his truck, and drove off the empty parking lot fading in the rearview mirror. Three days later, Josiah was at the kitchen table with a half-eaten peanut butter and jelly sandwich when tires crunched up the driveway.

Through the blinds, he saw Marsha step out of a silver SUV. A man in a suit followed, carrying a clipboard.

The knock was quick, businesslike.

Josiah opened the door.

"Josiah, this is Peter, my real estate agent," Marsha said, her tone clipped. "We're here to do a walkthrough."

Before he could speak, Peter was already measuring the living room with his eyes.

"What's going on?" Josiah asked, his voice tight.

Marsha didn't answer. She stepped past him, her heels clicking against the hardwood, and went straight to the kitchen window. "We'll put the 'For Sale' sign out front before we leave."

Josiah's chest tightened. "You couldn't even call first?"

"I told you, Josiah," she said, avoiding his eyes. "This house is going on the market."

Her gaze swept over the nearly bare walls. "Where's all of Marcus's stuff?"

"I gave some to your mother," he said quietly. "The rest... I couldn't keep looking at it every day."

Marsha's jaw tightened, but she didn't respond.

Peter was in the hallway, jotting notes. Marsha stepped closer to Josiah. "You'll need to be out before the first showing next week. I'll have the locks changed after that."

He stared at her. "So that's it? Eighteen years, and you just... cut me out?"

Her voice stayed cold. "I'm moving to California. I need a fresh start."

Josiah's hands shook. "What about the hearing for Marcus? You're not going?"

Marsha turned to face him fully for the first time. Her eyes glistened, but her voice was firm. "I buried my son once. I'm not sitting in a courtroom to watch them kill him again with a verdict I already know will come. I don't care what happens to that officer."

The words hit harder than any blow. For a moment, Josiah couldn't breathe.

Marsha stepped toward the door. "Goodbye, Josiah."

He didn't follow her. The sound of the front door shutting echoed through the empty house like a final judgment.

Through the window, he watched as Peter hammered the "For Sale" sign into the lawn. The metal stake went into the ground with three heavy thuds — each one landing in his chest.

The house was no longer his.

Soon, he wouldn't even have walls to pray inside.

# Chapter 10
## The Empty House

The house was too quiet.

Josiah stood in the front hallway, the morning light filtering through the blinds in pale streaks. Dust swirled lazily in the beams, floating without purpose, like his life now.

The coat hooks by the door still held Marcus's favorite hoodie, the gray one with the fading logo. The one he wore the day before he died. Josiah reached out and brushed his fingertips across the sleeve. The fabric was softer than he remembered, warm somehow, as if holding on to a piece of his son. His hand lingered, but the weight in his chest made it impossible to take it down.

The silence pressed against him from all sides. The walls, once alive with conversation and footsteps, now stood hollow, holding only echoes. Even the air felt stale. Josiah climbed the stairs slowly, each creak of the wood sounding like another goodbye. When he reached Marcus's bedroom door, he froze. It had stayed closed since that night.

His hand trembled as he reached for the knob. The metal felt cold, unforgiving.

The door groaned open.

Life, interrupted.

Marcus's room was frozen in time. A half-finished science project, a model heart made from plastic tubing waited patiently on the desk. His textbooks sat in an uneven tower, ready for the next study session that would never come. On the wall above his bed hung a list, written in his careful handwriting:

Become a pediatrician

Save enough for a microscope

Join the science club next year

Help someone who is scared at the hospital

Josiah's knees gave out. He sat heavily on the edge of the bed, pressing a hand over his mouth to keep from screaming. The sound wanted to rip out of him, wild and unrestrained, but he forced it down until it burned.

He should still be here. He should be looking at colleges, worrying about prom, complaining about exams not lying in a cold drawer, waiting for burial.

The air felt heavy, thick with memories. He reached for Marcus's backpack and slowly began packing.

The model heart.

His notebooks.

The list from the wall.

A half-used journal.

His lab goggles.

Each item felt like a piece of Marcus's future folded, zipped, and silenced.

When he finished, Josiah lowered himself onto the floor beside the bed. He placed his palm flat against the carpet, right where Marcus used to lie reading, humming softly to himself, toes wiggling when he solved a complex equation.

"I'm sorry, son," Josiah whispered. "I should've done more. I should've screamed louder. But I promise you, you will not be forgotten."

Tears blurred his vision as he kissed Marcus's pillow one last time and rose to his feet.

Downstairs, he scribbled a single sentence on a note and set it on the kitchen counter:

I can't breathe just like you, Marsha. I wish you well.

He placed his keys beside it, picked up his duffel bag, and looked around one last time.

"If she wants to sell it," he muttered, "she can finish cleaning it out."

When the door closed behind him, the sound was final.

Outside, the wind was picking up. The sky was the color of slate, promising rain. Josiah adjusted the strap of his duffel bag, turned toward the street, and started walking.

# Chapter 11
## The First Night

By nightfall, Josiah reached the east side of town. His feet ached, and the drizzle that had started hours ago had seeped into his clothes. The streetlamps flickered, casting pale light over cracked sidewalks.

Trinity Haven Men's Shelter stood ahead, a weathered brick building with a faded blue sign over the door. Warm light spilled from its windows, but it didn't feel like home. It felt like a place you ended up when you had nowhere else to go.

Inside, the air smelled faintly of disinfectant and old coffee. A man with tired eyes sat behind the intake desk.

"First time?" he asked gently.

Josiah nodded.

The man slid a clipboard across the counter. "Name?"

"Josiah Moore."

The pen felt heavy in his hand.

When the volunteer glanced up, recognition flickered in his eyes. "I'm... sorry about your son."

Josiah gave the slightest nod but said nothing. He didn't want pity. He wanted quiet.

The volunteer led him down a narrow hallway. Doors lined both sides, most closed. Somewhere down the hall, a TV murmured low news reports. A cough echoed from one of the rooms.

His assigned space was a small room in the far corner. A thin mattress lay on a metal cot. A single blanket was folded at the foot of the bed. The walls were barely concrete, painted an off-white that did little to brighten the space.

"It's not much," the man said. "But it's warm, and it locks."

"That's enough," Josiah replied quietly.

When the door closed, the silence was almost welcome. He set Marcus's backpack on the cot and unzipped it. The heart model came out first. He placed it on the nightstand, the red tubing catching the dim light from the small overhead bulb.

At the bottom of the bag, tucked between a sweatshirt and a notebook, he saw an envelope with his name written in Marsha's handwriting. His stomach tightened. He slid it out and turned it over in his hands.

He didn't open it. Not yet.

Instead, he slipped it under his pillow, lay back on the cot, and stared at the ceiling.

The room was cold. The mattress was hard. But after a long moment, Josiah let out a slow breath.

"Lord," he whispered, "I don't know what comes next. But I'm still here. And I still believe."

Rain tapped against the small window as he closed his eyes. Somewhere in the distance, a siren wailed.

Tonight, he was a man without a home. Tomorrow, he would be something else, though he didn't know what. Sleep didn't come right away.

The building had its own rhythm, a restless hum. Somewhere down the hall, a man coughed in a steady, hacking pattern. Doors opened and closed. Footsteps echoed off the hard tile. Two voices murmured in a conversation just loud enough to keep him from drifting off, followed by the sound of laughter that wasn't joyful, just tired.

Finally, he pushed the thin blanket aside and sat up. The air was cool against his skin, the cold that sinks in slowly until you feel it in your bones. He decided to get a drink of water.

The hall smelled faintly of disinfectant and burnt coffee. The kitchen was just a narrow room with a long counter, a few mismatched mugs, and a coffeepot that looked older than some of the men here.

"First night?" a voice asked.

Josiah turned. A man in his 50s sat at the table, stirring sugar into a steaming mug. His hair was gray at the temples, his clothes clean but worn thin.

"Yeah," Josiah said quietly.

The man nodded, as if that explained everything. "Name's Rick. I have been here five months. Don't let the place get to you, it's better than the street. Curfew's strict, breakfast is bad, and if you can get work, get it quick. They'll push you out if you don't."

Josiah gave a slight nod, not trusting himself to say more.

Rick kept talking, like he'd learned the silence of new arrivals didn't mean disinterest. "Some guys get back on their feet. Others... they get stuck. Don't be one of the stuck ones."

Josiah managed a faint, "I won't."

On the way back to his room, he passed two men in the hallway, their voices raised in a heated argument. A staff member stepped between them, hands out, his voice calm but firm. The tension crackled in the air. Josiah kept walking, head down, until he was back in the small, dim space that was now his.

He sat on the cot, pulled Marcus's hoodie from the backpack, and pressed it to his face. The scent was faint of detergent, shampoo, something warm and familiar, but it was enough to pull the ache in his chest wide open again.

Curling up, he pulled the hoodie over his head, tucking the sleeves close around his neck. He slid the thin blanket over himself, but the cold still seeped in.

On the nightstand, the heart model seemed to watch him.

His eyes drifted to the edge of the pillow where a folded envelope peeked out. Marsha's handwriting. He stared at it for a long time, his breath shallow.

Not tonight, he told himself.

He turned onto his other side, pulling the blanket tighter. Rain began to tap against the small window, a steady rhythm that should have been comforting. But every few minutes, the sound faded into Marcus's voice in his head and each time, Josiah's eyes snapped open, to remember the boy wasn't there.

# Chapter 12
## The Letter

The rain had stopped sometime in the night.

When Josiah woke, the light through the small window was dim and gray, the kind of morning that feels like it never fully arrives. The air was still cool, and the quiet inside the shelter was different now, less restless, more resigned.

He sat up slowly, the thin blanket sliding off his shoulders. Marcus's hoodie was still wrapped around him, the sleeves knotted loosely at his chest. The heart model sat on the nightstand, catching the pale light like something fragile, like hope.

He reached for the backpack, meaning only to put the hoodie away. That's when he saw it again, the folded envelope under the pillow, the handwriting he knew as well as his name.

Marsha.

His chest tightened.

Last night, he'd told himself he wasn't ready. But this morning, he realized there would never be a "ready."

He picked up the letter, turning it in his hands. The paper was soft from being handled, the edges slightly bent. He stared at her name in the corner until the lines blurred, then unfolded it.

*Dear Josiah,*

*I've written this letter a hundred times in my head, but I never had the strength to put it into words until now.*

*If you're reading this, it's because I finally found the courage to tell you the truth: not just about why I left, but about what was breaking inside me long before I walked away.*

*The day we lost Marcus, everything inside me shattered. I can't describe the kind of pain that lived in my bones after that. It wasn't just grief it was guilt, emptiness, and a silence that screamed at me every moment. I couldn't breathe in that house anymore. Every room held pieces of him... his laughter, his footsteps, his science materials scattered across the floor. And every single piece hurt.*

*But the most challenging part, Josiah, was the space that grew between you and me.*

*You were grieving in your way quiet, strong, focused, but I needed something else. I needed you to fall apart with me, to hold me when I collapsed in the hallway, to scream with me at the unfairness of it all.*

*Instead, we became strangers standing on opposite ends of the same heartbreak, unable to reach each other.*

*I didn't leave because I stopped loving you.*

*I left because I didn't know how to love you through that kind of pain. Every time I looked into your eyes, I saw Marcus. And I saw all the words we weren't saying.*

*It was like trying to build a bridge with broken hands.*

*I didn't know how to heal. And I didn't know how to help you heal either.*

*So, I ran.*

*I thought maybe if I left, we could both start to breathe again. Perhaps the space would help us find our way back to ourselves, even if we never found our way back to each other.*

*I think about you every day.*

*I wonder if you hate me, or if you understand. I hope, more than anything, that you've found some peace. Marcus would want that. He'd like us to live, even if it's without him… and even if it's apart.*

*I'm not asking for forgiveness, Josiah. I'm just asking for understanding.*

*I loved you then.*

*I love you still.*

*And a part of me always will.*

*With all my heart,*

*Marsha*

Josiah didn't move for a long time. The letter trembled in his hands, as if the weight of her words had cracked something deep inside him. He read it once. Then again. And now it just lay open in his lap, like an exposed wound.

Her handwriting was so achingly familiar with the curves, the loops, the little way she crossed her "t's." It was almost unbearable to look at.

She left because she was drowning, too.

It wasn't anger that rose in his chest not anymore. It was something heavier, something hollow, a grief within the grief. For the first time, he understood they hadn't just lost Marcus, they had lost each other in the wreckage of that loss.

I needed you to fall apart with me.

The words echoed in his mind like a ghost.

He thought back to those nights when she'd sat alone on the edge of the bed, shoulders shaking, while he lay beside her, staring at the ceiling, silent, thinking strength meant holding it in. Thinking it was what they both needed.

But maybe strength isn't always quiet.

Maybe real strength is screaming in the room together. Perhaps it's holding your wife when she's falling apart, even if you feel like you're dying inside too.

Tears welled, and this time, he didn't wipe them away. He let them fall. For Marcus. For Marsha. For himself.

He whispered her name like a prayer.

And for the first time in years, Josiah broke not just as a father who had lost a son, but as a man who had lost the love of his life to the same storm that had taken everything else.

And then came the deepest ache of all.

What if I had just reached for her sooner?

# Chapter 13
## Shadows at the Courthouse

The courthouse steps were a sea of noise.

Cardboard signs swayed in the winter wind,

JUSTICE FOR MARCUS was painted in bold strokes beside others declaring SUPPORT OUR POLICE. Reporters huddled under umbrellas, cameras aimed at the entrance, their microphones bristling with foam covers damp from drizzle.

Josiah kept his head low, collar pulled high, slipping in through the side door where the sheriff's deputy barely glanced up from his clipboard. The scent of wet coats and cold coffee hit him as soon as he entered the security line. His shoes squeaked against the marble floor, the sound far too loud in his ears.

He avoided the elevator, taking the stairs instead, counting each step like it might keep his thoughts from unraveling.

Inside the courtroom, the hum of conversation cut short when the bailiff called for order. Josiah found a seat in the last row, near the far wall. From here, no one could see the way his hands shook.

The trial began with procedural motions, the sort of legal chatter that blurred together, until the prosecutor called the first witness, a teacher from Marcus's school. She spoke in short, clipped phrases, her voice steady but her knuckles white.

"We heard the first shots from the math wing. I locked my classroom door and moved the students to the back wall. Some were crying. One... one asked if they were going to die."

Josiah's jaw tightened. He closed his eyes, and for an instant, he saw Marcus in that hallway, looking for safety, trusting that help would come.

Next came a paramedic. He described arriving on the scene, weaving past crying parents and police tape. "We triaged. There were... multiple victims. The boy we found near the gym..."

Josiah's stomach twisted. The paramedic's voice dipped lower. "He wasn't breathing when we got there."

No one said Marcus's name. Not once.

By midday, the judge called for a recess. Josiah stayed seated while others filed out, reporters rushing for the hallway to broadcast updates. He stared at the empty witness stand, the polished wood catching the courtroom lights.

He knew the next session would be harder. Officer Johnson was on the witness list.

Outside, chants grew louder, vibrating through the glass windows.

Justice for the children.

Protect those who protect us.

Two sides shouting past each other, not knowing the father of the dead boy was sitting alone, just a few feet away.

# Chapter 14
## The Weight of the Verdict

When the gavel fell, everyone stood. Officer Johnson walked in from the side room, his uniform traded for a suit that didn't fit his shoulders. He moved stiffly, as if each step cost him.

The prosecutor approached.

"How long had you been on the force?"

"Nine months."

"What training did you have for active shooter scenarios?"

Johnson answered in clipped, practiced lines—academy drills, safety protocols, the checklists they all memorized. Then came the moment his voice faltered.

"But nothing prepared me for that day."

He recounted the call, the chaos, the locked hallways. "I came around the corner by the gym... and I saw someone. I reacted. I fired."

The prosecutor leaned in. "You didn't issue a warning?"

"No."

"You didn't confirm if it was a threat?"

"No."

"Do you know who it was you shot?"

"Yes." His voice broke. "A child."

Josiah's grip on the bench in front of him tightened until his knuckles went pale.

When cross-examination ended, the judge called another recess. Josiah drifted to a window at the far end of the hall. The chants outside were clearer now, sharp and divided.

"You're a murderer!"

"He's a hero!"

Two truths, depending on which sign you held.

Back in the courtroom, closing arguments cut like glass.

The prosecutor: "A child is dead because Officer Johnson ignored his training."

The defense: "This was a tragedy, not a crime."

The jury left to deliberate. Minutes passed. Hours. Josiah stayed in his seat, invisible to all.

When the jurors filed back in, the air was brittle.

"We, the jury, find the defendant guilty of Count One of manslaughter."

Gasps. Silence.

The judge thanked the jury and struck the gavel. The court adjourned.

Josiah slipped out with the others, brushing past a reporter who didn't even glance at him. On the courthouse steps, protestors cheered and cursed in equal measure. He walked through them like smoke, unseen, unheard. Josiah walked aimlessly, letting his feet decide where to go. The cold air cut through his jacket, sharper than it had that morning. He passed storefronts he used to visit with Marcus, corner diners, a hardware shop, the bakery where his son had once insisted on picking the biggest cookie. Every window seemed to reflect a man he didn't recognize.

His stomach growled, but his pockets had less cash these few days. He knew that every dollar counted. When he pulled out his phone to call Marsha, the screen flashed, No Service. The bill hadn't been paid.

He stopped at a small cell phone shop, the kind with faded posters in the window. The clerk barely looked up when Josiah asked for the cheapest prepaid phone.

"That'll get you a few weeks," the man said, sliding the box across the counter. Josiah handed over crumpled bills and left, the bell above the door ringing hollow.

Outside, the wind picked up. He spotted a bus idling at the corner and climbed aboard. The driver glanced at him, then waved him through without asking for a fare.

The ride was short. The shelter's sign flickered, one bulb out, the others buzzing faintly. He hesitated on the steps, hearing the muffled clatter of trays and low conversation inside.

Dinner was being served. It was mashed potatoes, meatloaf, green beans. The food smelled faintly of onions, and something burnt.

Josiah picked up a tray and scanned the crowded room. Some tables were loud with laughter; others were silent, eyes fixed on plates.

An older man sat alone near the back, his tray untouched.

"Mind if I sit here?" Josiah asked.

The man looked up, eyes measuring him. "Not at all. I'm Frank."

"Josiah."

"You new here?" Frank asked between bites.

"Yeah. Just hit a rough patch," Josiah admitted. "But it'll get better."

Frank smirked without humor. "I've been saying that for five years."

They ate slowly, trading pieces of their stories of loss, regrets, small victories that didn't last.

And yet, as Josiah listened, something flickered inside him. While Frank spoke about the shelter's broken plumbing and the kids who came in hungry after school, Josiah's mind was already sketching ideas of job programs, after-school meals, community rebuilding.

He had no job. No savings. No home. But he still had something left.

Hope.

It wasn't much. But it was enough to start.

# Chapter 15
## The Streets

Four months at the shelter had taught Josiah two things: keep your head down and guard your spot like your life depended on it. He'd managed to save $200, not much, but enough to feel like he was inching forward.

Every day there was a grind. Mornings started with coffee that tasted like burnt cardboard, followed by hours in the resource room, filling out online applications that seemed to vanish into thin air. Construction manager, foreman, site supervisor, jobs he was more than qualified for. But no one called.

Some nights, he'd lie in his narrow bunk, staring at the ceiling, wondering if employers Googled his name and saw the news coverage of Marcus's death. Maybe they thought he was troubled. Perhaps they just didn't care.

That morning, Josiah settled into his usual computer station. The screen flickered twice before loading. He started an application for a construction manager position across town, his fingers moving slower than normal. His stomach growled, he'd skipped breakfast to get here early.

The door to the resource room banged open.

"Hey, man," Frank said, slightly out of breath. "I got something. A company needs painters.... today only. Seventy-five bucks cash. You in?"

Josiah hesitated. He needed to keep job-hunting. But seventy-five dollars meant bus fare, a hot meal, maybe a new pair of socks.

"Alright," he said finally. "Let's go." Josiah, Frank, and a few other men from the shelter loaded up the van to go to the jobsite. Once there, they painted several rooms inside an office building on the south side of the city. Time slipped away. When they looked up, it was well past 5 p.m.

"We need to leave!" Josiah called out. "We'll lose our beds at the shelter."

The other men dropped their brushes and rushed outside, only to discover the van was gone.

Frank ran to the contractor's trailer. The man inside looked up from the blueprints.

"The driver left. Family emergency," he said casually.

"How are we supposed to get back?" Frank demanded.

"I don't know. I can't transport ten people."

You used us for cheap labor, and now you're leaving us stranded? That's not right!"

The crowd erupted in anger, voices overlapping in outrage.

Josiah raised his hands, urging them to calm down. "Let's walk."

No one wanted to, but there was no other choice.

As they walked, Josiah tried to view it like a camping trip through the wilderness. He enjoyed the scenery, even though he wished he could run with the younger men. He didn't want to leave Frank behind.

"At least it's not winter," Frank joked. "Otherwise, we'd be sleeping in that trailer."

Josiah chuckled.

Eventually, they found a small park about fifteen miles from the city, hidden behind a grove of trees. It had benches, picnic tables, and a covered shelter.

"Why don't we just sleep here for the night?" one man suggested. "We'll have a roof if it rains."

It wasn't ideal. The benches were hard, the air was cool, and distant traffic interrupted their thoughts. Josiah couldn't sleep. Frank noticed the look on his face…. Josiah wasn't used to rock bottom.

Trying to lighten the mood, Frank swapped stories about past jobs and joked about their "camping trip." Others joined in, vowing never to work for that company again.

By the time dawn broke, the men were exhausted, but they were also more connected to one another. They had made it through the night. When they heard a bus approaching in the distance, they laughed in relief.

Their unexpected camping adventure had come to an end. It wasn't just a rough night, it was a moment of shared resilience. As they climbed aboard the bus back to the shelter, Josiah felt a little more hopeful.

He didn't have much. But he had Frank. And for now, that was enough.

# Chapter 16
## Nowhere to Go

Once they arrived back at the homeless shelter, the case manager was waiting for them in the lobby, her arms folded tightly across her chest.

"Where have you all been?" she demanded.

Josiah and the others exchanged uneasy glances.

"We got stranded," one man explained. "The company didn't bring us back like they said."

Her eyes narrowed. "That's exactly why I told you to check in if you were going to be late. Now, we've had to give away your beds. Rules are rules." She grabbed the phone and dialed the company's owner.

Josiah listened as she launched into a sharp, unwavering complaint, detailing the abandonment and demanding that the crew never set foot on shelter property again. The call ended with a clipped, "You're banned."

That should have felt like justice, but it didn't.

"Can I at least get my belongings?" Josiah asked.

The case manager gestured toward the hall. "Make it quick."

Inside the small room, Josiah's heart dropped. His duffel bag had been unzipped and rummaged through. Several shirts and pants were missing. His shaving kit and soap.... gone. It was as if someone had carved away the last slivers of dignity he owned.

He stuffed what was left into the bag and walked outside.

Frank was leaning against a trash can, peering into a greasy paper bag, pulling out half a sandwich.

"Frank," Josiah said quietly, "put that down. I've got a couple of bucks. Let's go get something real."

Frank's eyes lit up, and he tossed the sandwich back in.

They walked in silence for a few blocks. Josiah's mind churned. *A year ago, I was driving my truck to my job sites. Now I'm counting change for fast food.*

Frank must have noticed the heaviness in his footsteps. "You gonna make it through this?"

Josiah managed a thin smile. "I'm not giving up. I need to eat."

Inside the restaurant, they ordered two small sandwiches and sat in the corner. Josiah leaned forward. "We didn't even get paid for yesterday."

Frank snorted. "Yeah. They pulled that stunt on me last year, too. Welcome to the streets, brother."

Josiah exhaled slowly. "I need something steady. Any other shelters around?"

Frank shrugged. "There's one, but you gotta line up by four every day, and it's an open bay.... no walls, no privacy. But you eat better."

It became their pattern.... lining up at one shelter, crashing on a church basement floor, or sharing a park bench when there were no beds left.

Some nights, Josiah's stomach cramped so badly from hunger that he couldn't sleep. He learned where the food trucks parked on Fridays, which dumpsters held the least-spoiled leftovers, and which convenience stores would look the other way if he filled a cup with water.

One afternoon, he tried for a job interview. He'd scrubbed his shirt in a public restroom and dried it under a hand dryer, but when he walked into the office, the receptionist wrinkled her nose. The manager didn't even shake his hand before saying, "We'll call you," and ushering him out.

The rejection stung worse than the hunger.

A week later, he sat in the employment center lobby, clutching a paper ticket with the number 24. He got up to wash his face in the restroom, scrubbing with the tiny bar of motel soap he kept wrapped in a napkin.

When he came back, the receptionist called, "Number 27."

Josiah's heart sank. "I just missed it. Can you still see me today?"

"No," she said flatly. "Come back tomorrow."

He walked outside, fists clenched. The sky was gray and heavy. "Why, Lord?" he whispered. "How much lower can I go?"

A raindrop struck his cheek. Then another. Within seconds, the sky opened up.

He ducked under an awning and froze. It was his old office building. Only now, the glass door bore a new name: Sweet Haven Bakery.

Through the window, he saw warm lighting, the swirl of cinnamon rolls in the oven, and smiling faces over coffee.

The door opened, and a woman in an apron stepped out. "Sir, you're blocking the entrance. We don't do handouts. You'll need to move along."

"I'm just trying to stay dry," Josiah said quietly.

Her smile didn't change. "Move along."

He stepped back into the rain. A passing garbage truck sprayed him with muddy water. His knees buckled, and he sank to the sidewalk, covering his face.

Somewhere in the rain, a voice echoed in his spirit: "Get up."

He looked around. No one was there.

By the time he made it back to the shelter, the line was complete.

"Try the community center with the red door and pink bricks," the staffer said.

Three blocks later, soaked and shivering, Josiah collapsed under an oak tree in a small park.

The next morning, a fever burned through him, and every breath rattled. By the time the shelter staff found him and called EMS, Josiah could barely stand.

The doctor's voice was muffled behind a mask. "You've tested positive for COVID-19. Pneumonia's already set in. You'll be in isolation."

The days blurred. The oxygen mask, IV drips, the constant hiss of machines.

On the fifth day, a nurse wheeled in a small TV. "Figured you'd want something to watch. Big case on the news."

Josiah's heart thudded. Marcus.

The courtroom filled the screen with reporters, tense faces, and the jury shuffling back into their seats. The judge asked for the verdict.

The foreman's voice was steady. "Guilty on all counts."

Josiah's chest tightened not from the illness, but from relief. Tears welled in his eyes.

The camera cut to the crowd outside, still protesting. Signs lifted. Voices shouted. Justice had come, but it felt distant from this sterile hospital room.

He leaned back against the pillow. Even in his storm, God had been moving.

"I'm still here," he whispered. "And so is He."

# Chapter 17
# Long Road Back

Josiah walked a few blocks from the hospital, still weak but breathing on his own. Each step was a reminder of how far he had come. He was grateful to be alive.

As he reached the bus stop, a TV in the corner of a small storefront caught his eye. A crowd was gathered, watching the news. The headline scrolled across the bottom again; it was on every channel for days: "Michael Johnson Verdict: Guilty."

Josiah stood for a moment, listening to the reporter describe the courtroom's tense atmosphere and the protests still raging outside. A part of him wished he could've been there, but the streets had their own demands. He whispered a quiet prayer for him and his family before turning toward the bench.

"Hey Frank," Josiah said, voice hoarse.

Frank looked up, eyes widening. "Josiah! Man, I haven't seen you at the hangouts. Where've you been?"

"I just got out of the hospital. COVID-19," Josiah replied, lowering himself carefully onto the bench.

"Man, that's rough. I'm glad to see you on your feet. How are you feeling?"

"I'm better. Still a little weak. They gave me some sample meds and an inhaler. Thank God they didn't send me off with prescriptions I couldn't afford to fill."

Frank nodded solemnly. "Yeah, prescriptions these days will cost you your last meal. You heading to the shelter?"

"Yeah. Hoping to get a bed. I can't be out here tonight, not like this."

The bus pulled up. Frank asked the driver if they could ride for free, explaining they were heading to the shelter. The driver agreed, and they climbed aboard.

As they rode, Josiah leaned against the window. "You always seem to know someone, Frank. That bus ride just saved me ten blocks of pain."

Frank gave a half-smile. "When you've been around the streets as long as I have, you start to build up a network. Sometimes, it's the little favors that get us through."

When they reached the shelter, Josiah asked Mr. Richardson if there were any available beds.

"Sorry, buddy," Mr. Richardson said. "We filled up three days ago. Where've you been?"

"I was in the hospital," Josiah explained.

"Oh man. I'm sorry to hear that, but we're full."

Mr. Richardson turned to Frank. "And you?"

"I had to visit my second love," Frank said with a grin.

Josiah raised an eyebrow. "Second love?"

Frank chuckled. "An old spot I go to for peace. Let's say she doesn't talk back and always gives me a view."

They ate a quick meal at the shelter, then left. Night had fallen. The streets were quiet. They made their way to Harmony Creek Park, their familiar fallback.

As they walked, Frank told old stories to lift Josiah's spirits.

"Remember that guy with the pigeon who thought he was training it to deliver mail?" Frank asked, chuckling.

Josiah smiled weakly. "Yeah. He swore it brought back messages from his ex-wife."

Frank laughed. "It just kept flying back to the same bench. Man, we've seen some things."

Josiah nodded but said little. Sleeping outside again after having a real bed stung.

Frank noticed the silence. "Remember, Josiah, we've been through worse. We'll find a way to make it."

They reached the park. The bench was cold, but familiar. They used their jackets as makeshift blankets and huddled close for warmth.

The morning came quickly. Josiah groaned from the stiffness. "My back is killing me," he muttered as he stood slowly.

They returned to the shelter hoping for a shower and breakfast. They managed to wash up and then headed to the dining hall. Frank spotted an old friend and went to greet him, leaving Josiah alone.

As Josiah ate slowly, a man loomed over him.

"You going to eat that muffin?" the man asked.

Josiah looked up. "Yes. I am."

The man reached for the muffin. Josiah snatched it away.

"What's wrong with you?" he snapped. "Leave me alone."

"I'm hungry," the man muttered.

"So go through the line again," Josiah barked. His blood boiled. "Not today, Satan. Not today."

He stood and left the dining hall.

Outside, Frank noticed Josiah's mood and quickly followed.

"You good, man?" Frank asked.

"I'm just tired. Tired of all of it," Josiah replied.

They walked together in silence. Josiah's mind was flooded with everything he had endured—the pain, the loss, the helplessness.

Eventually, they found a quiet spot in a small park. Frank sat beside him, silent and supportive.

Josiah finally broke the silence. "I can't keep living like this, Frank. I'm suffocating."

Frank nodded. "I know. Let's try the shelter on the west side. It's a few blocks from here."

They made their way there. Inside, Frank was greeted by Ms. Wells, a long-term supporter.

"Frank, it's been a while. How are you?"

"I'm alright. My friend Josiah has just been released from the hospital. We've been to three shelters. We need a place to stay."

Ms. Wells saw the desperation in their eyes. "Let me check with my supervisor. Have a seat."

They waited twenty minutes. Then came the verdict.... no beds. Back on the street again.

Over the following weeks, Josiah and Frank drifted between shelters, churches, and warming centers. They often had to hide in bathrooms overnight, only to be kicked out in the morning.

Their spirits began to wane. Josiah clung to fragments of hope, but the weight of rejection, violence, and hunger pressed on him daily.

Some nights, they got lucky, a church opened its doors, or a kind stranger handed them leftovers. Other nights were colder, crueler.

One day, they discovered a small shelter. It was clean. It wasn't permanent, but it offered meals and a few hours of rest.

It became a small oasis.

While there, Josiah was cleaning out his bag when a group of men approached.

"Can I get one of those care bags?" one man asked.

"I'm sorry. No," Josiah replied.

Without warning, the man punched Josiah in the face. Another grabbed his hygiene bag and wallet. Josiah fell, unable to fight back. His eye swelled. His nose bled.

Frank rushed over. "What happened?"

"They jumped me. Took my stuff."

Frank shook his head. "We're all struggling, but this? This is savage."

Josiah winced. "We don't need to hurt each other to survive."

They left the shelter and returned to the streets.

The days grew colder. Josiah developed a persistent cough. Every gust of wind stung his face.

"I just need to get through the winter," he thought. "Maybe the shelter will open up."

Each day brought new challenges. Some strangers were kind, offering food or warm coffee. Others were cruel or indifferent.

On a frigid morning, a woman handed Josiah a pair of gloves. "You look like you could use these more than I can," she said with a kind smile.

"Thank you," Josiah whispered, moved almost to tears.

But those moments were rare. The cold reality of his situation was always waiting for him.

Still, Josiah kept walking.

One step at a time.

Toward something better.

# Chapter 18
## The Bird's Nest

"Oh, my back hurts," Josiah groaned as he tried to sit up on the bench. The wood creaked under him, stiff with dew. His shoulders ached from the chill that had settled into his bones overnight. The damp air carried the scent of wet earth, exhaust fumes from the nearby road, and the faint, sour smell of trash. Far-off traffic murmured like a restless ocean.

He rubbed his eyes, gritting his teeth as he stretched, feeling the ache ripple down his spine. Years of sleeping on hard ground had shaped his mornings into battles each awakening a small war. But these last few months had been the worst. Recovery from illness while still surviving the streets had left him more worn down than ever.

He rose slowly, testing his legs. His stomach tightened painfully, reminding him he hadn't eaten the night before. His mouth was dry, his skin greasy from days without a proper wash. He headed toward the shelter, craving his usual routine of a shower, food, and the thin thread of dignity it offered.

Inside, the fluorescent lights buzzed overhead. The case manager, Mr. Richardson, stood at the counter, sorting donated clothes.

"How are you doing today, Josiah?" he asked with a steady voice.

"Yeah, I've had better days," Josiah admitted.

"Remain patient; your better days are at hand," Mr. Richardson encouraged. "Hang in there, buddy. It'll likely be another two weeks before a permanent bed becomes available. But here, take some extra clothing and two carry bags."

"I greatly appreciate it," Josiah said. "Any chance you can spare a room tonight? Just as an emergency?"

Mr. Richardson hesitated. "Let me check with my supervisor. We've got new parolees coming in tomorrow for the pre-release program, so space is tight."

A short while later, Mr. Richardson found him in the dining hall. "I'm sorry, man. I couldn't get you a bed. But here's a list of other shelters that might have space."

"It's alright," Josiah replied, though disappointment tugged at him. "I'll figure it out."

After dinner, Josiah asked for a to-go bag, thinking ahead to breakfast. Outside, his usual bench was already taken. He looked at the shelter list. The closest available bed was more than 30 minutes away, too far without bus fare.

He sighed, then thought of "The Bird's Nest" an encampment a few blocks away, tucked behind a row of abandoned buildings.

The Bird's Nest wasn't much to look at, an uneven patch of ground littered with crushed cans, plastic bags, and broken bottles. Makeshift tents sagged between trees, patched together with tarps, duct tape, and sheets of plywood. Smoke from a small fire pit curled into the night air. The place had its own rhythm, its own unspoken rules.

He found a spot behind a dumpster where a stained mattress sat, smelling of mildew and worse. Every instinct told him not to touch it, but the thought of lying on bare concrete was worse.

"Every time I come here, I have to keep my bags close," he muttered, tucking them under his head. "Things tend to grow legs out here."

He was almost asleep when voices shattered the quiet.

"Hey, that's mine!" a man shouted.

"No, it's not. I saw it first," another snapped.

Josiah pushed himself up. Two men stood over a large piece of cardboard, gripping opposite ends like it was gold. The older man's hands trembled; the younger's jaw was tight.

"It's not just cardboard," the older man said through clenched teeth. "It keeps the cold from crawling into your bones."

The younger man shot back, "I've been sleeping on wet ground for a week. This is the first dry thing I've seen."

Josiah stepped forward, irritation and sadness mixing in his chest. "We're out here fighting over something most people would throw away."

The younger man's eyes narrowed. "Easy for you to say when you're not the one freezing to death."

Josiah glanced at the older man, then back at the younger. "I've been freezing for years. But if you fight over everything, you'll lose more than you gain. Take it and move along."

The young man hesitated, then yanked the cardboard free and walked away muttering. Josiah turned back toward his mattress and froze. One of his bags was gone.

His pulse jumped. "That had my extra clothes and food." He scanned the shadows, asking the nearby campers if they'd seen anything. They avoided his eyes.

He sat back down, anger knotting in his gut. "There's no grace out here," he thought.

Sleep was impossible. Hours passed, each minute grinding on his nerves. When dawn came, he left the filthy sheet behind and started toward the shelter. That's when he saw her.

A woman lay motionless near a trash pile, her skin dark and ashy, her body still. The stench of decay drifted on the breeze.

Josiah's breath caught. "Is she...?" He stepped closer, his chest tightening. Memories of his own illness, of nights spent wondering if he'd wake in the morning, flashed through him.

A man pushing a shopping cart rattled past. Josiah stopped him. "Hey, can you call someone? I think this woman might be dead."

The man's face was unreadable. "Happens all the time. Bridges, alleys, tents. Overdoses. People just... don't wake up."

Josiah's voice cracked. "She's still a person."

The man shrugged and kept moving.

Josiah stood there for a moment, staring at her. "Lord, why is this the world we live in?" he whispered. "Why do we let people slip away like they don't matter?"

His throat burned. Finally, he turned and kept walking. "Nothing changes unless someone decides to change it," he told himself.

Back on the main road, Josiah stopped and whispered, "There's no way our community believes a life is worth nothing just because of hardship." He covered his mouth, eyes filled with disbelief. "But I must continue," he told himself. "Nothing changes unless someone decides to change it." He walked several blocks until he was back at the shelter. Once inside, he reported what he'd seen. The front desk clerk nodded and made the call.

Josiah stayed in the lobby a while longer, waiting for Mr. Richardson to finish intake. The noise of the shelter faded into the background as his thoughts returned to the woman he had seen at the Bird's Nest. He couldn't shake the image of her stillness, the quiet surrender in the way she lay.

"This world can make you forget you're worth something," he thought, tightening his grip on the strap of his remaining backpack.

When Mr. Richardson finally waved him over, Josiah retook the list of resources. "I'll try some of these tomorrow," he said, forcing a small smile.

Outside, the evening air wrapped around him like a heavy blanket. He walked back toward the park, passing the familiar streets that had become both a map and a prison. He found his usual bench empty this time, and he sank onto it, setting his backpack beside him.

He bowed his head. The city noise blurred into a distant hum as he prayed. "Lord… help me to stand in this. Help me not to forget who I am…. and who You are…. even when I'm overlooked, even when I'm tired. Even when I feel invisible."

A soft breeze rustled through the trees, and for a moment, the air felt lighter. Josiah opened his eyes. Nothing about his situation had changed — but something inside him had.

He was still here. Still breathing and still believing.

# Chapter 19

## A Bed for the Night

The next morning, Josiah woke early, as he always did, no matter where he laid his head. Last night, he'd found a quiet patch of grass by a small waterfall in the state park. The sound of rushing water had lulled him into an uneasy sleep. Now, the damp earth carried a chill, clinging to his clothes and bones. The first rays of sunlight stretched across the park, and the distant hum of traffic reminded him that the city was already moving.

He rubbed the stiffness from his neck and gathered his belongings. One bag went on his back, another in front. The tote bag hung on his forearm, heavy from what little he owned. He left before a park officer could fine him for sleeping in the park. As much as the waterfall had been a peaceful refuge for the night, he knew there was no safety in staying too long.

When he reached the shelter, Mr. Richardson's voice greeted him like a long-lost friend.

"Finally, Josiah, we have a bed available!"

Josiah stopped, the words sinking in. His hands trembled as he set his bags down and fell to his knees right in the lobby.

"Thank You, Jesus," he whispered. Relief swept through him in warm waves. It wasn't a hotel suite. It wasn't home. But it was a roof over his head and for tonight, that was everything.

The shelter sat in a forgotten part of town, where sidewalks were cracked, streetlights flickered, and stray cats wandered without fear. The brick building's paint had long since faded, but inside it offered something rare: a small measure of safety for those who had nowhere else to go.

Mr. Richardson motioned toward the elevator.

"Come on, let's get you settled."

During the slow ride to the third floor, Josiah thanked him for keeping his name on the list for so long. He'd missed a few chances for a permanent bed in the past, mostly because life on the street didn't come with reliable schedules.

"Oh, I forgot to tell you," Mr. Richardson said suddenly. "Frank's body was found in the Bird's Nest last week."

Josiah froze. "What? How did he die?"

"Overdose," Richardson replied, his voice low. "I didn't know Frank did drugs either, but… he'd been struggling for years. He used to work at the nuclear plant with my father until an injury took him out. Back surgery led to painkillers. Then street drugs. He spent his money on his "high" instead of his mortgage. Lost the house. Lost his wife and kids. She left town with their boys."

Josiah's stomach tightened. "How old was he?"

"About seventy-one. Said his addiction was his 'second love.'"

Josiah shook his head. "He was my friend."

Richardson sighed. "I thought you should know. I know you two were close."

The elevator dinged. The door opened to a hallway lined with numbered doors and dim ceiling lights. Richardson led him to a small room and unlocked the door.

"Here you go, buddy. I hope things start turning around for you."

"I believe they will. God will make a way," Josiah said. He laid his bags beside the bed and sank into the thin mattress. It felt like heaven.

When he opened his eyes again, Mr. Richardson was knocking.

"Dinner in fifteen."

Josiah jolted upright. He'd slept almost eight hours. After lacing his shoes, he headed downstairs. The dining hall smelled of warm bread and seasoned stew, making his stomach growl. As he ate, thoughts of Frank lingered the streets had claimed another life.

After dinner, Josiah returned to his room. The hum of the building was strangely comforting. He thought about Frank's laugh, the way he'd always share a scrap of food, and how quickly a life could disappear. Tomorrow was uncertain, but tonight he was indoors. Tonight, he was safe.

He whispered a prayer of thanks and closed his eyes, unaware that the morning would bring a face from his past.

# Chapter 20
## Ghosts From the Past

The next morning, Josiah woke feeling more rested than he had in months. His back still ached from years of concrete and park benches, but the thin mattress had been a small mercy. He stretched, listening to the muffled sounds of the shelter waking, footsteps in the hall, the creak of pipes, the low hum of voices carrying through the vents.

A faint smell of instant coffee and toast pulled him downstairs. He picked up a tray of oatmeal, toast, and a small carton of milk and scanned the dining room for a place to sit.

That's when he saw him.

At a corner table, hunched over his plate, was a man Josiah hadn't seen in years. His hair was shorter, his frame thinner, his shoulders sloped in a way that spoke of time served. But the face...that face... was burned into Josiah's memory.

Officer Johnson.

For a moment, Josiah froze. The man who had pulled the trigger that ended Marcus's life was here, in the same room, eating the same complimentary breakfast.

Balancing his tray, Josiah walked toward him, each step feeling heavier than the last.

"Is that you... Officer Johnson?"

The man looked up, startled. His eyes were sunken, rimmed with sleepless nights. "I'm not a police officer anymore," he said quietly. "Just... an ex-con. Just call me, Michael."

Josiah swallowed hard. "What happened?"

"I served five years," Johnson replied, staring down at his plate. "For taking a child's life during a school incident. Accidental, they said, but the jury... well, you know how that went." His voice cracked. "I didn't mean to. I never meant to."

Josiah's chest tightened. He could feel his pulse in his ears. "The boy you shot... Marcus Moore... was my son."

Johnson's fork slipped from his hand, clattering against the tray. He stared at Josiah, his lips parting like he'd been punched. "Your... son?"

Josiah nodded slowly, the words tasting like iron.

Johnson's face crumpled. "I... I can't even say his name without choking. In prison, I wrote it down a hundred times. Sometimes I'd wake up hearing it. Sometimes... I wished I wouldn't wake up at all."

The rawness in his voice caught Josiah off guard. He'd replayed this meeting in his mind for years, imagined shouting, imagined walking away, imagined never speaking to the man at all. But standing here, he saw not the uniform, not the authority, but a broken man drowning in guilt.

Josiah took a deep breath. His faith whispered from somewhere deep inside: If you hold on to the anger, you'll never heal.

"I forgive you," he said.

Johnson's head jerked up. "You... forgive me?"

"Yes. It doesn't erase what happened, and it doesn't mean I don't miss my boy every day. But I can't live with hate rotting me from the inside. My son wouldn't want that for me. God wouldn't want that for me."

Johnson's lips trembled. "You're giving me more grace than I gave your son that day."

The words hit like a hammer, but Josiah didn't flinch. "Grace is the only way forward."

They sat in silence for a while after that, the clinking of silverware around them a faint reminder that life moved on whether either of them was ready or not.

Later that morning, Josiah returned to his room, the conversation still echoing in his mind. But before he could close the door, two shelter staff members appeared in the hallway with clipboards.

"Room check," one of them said briskly.

Josiah stepped aside as they came in, moving through his space with methodical precision, checking under the bed, inside the closet, lifting the mattress.

One of them glanced at him. "Random inspection. We had some issues last month, stolen food, drugs, even a few weapons. We can't risk it happening again."

Josiah nodded, arms crossed, watching them work. He had nothing to hide, but the intrusion felt heavy all the same.

When they left, the room felt smaller. He sat on the edge of his bed, the image of Officer Johnson's tear-streaked face flashing in his mind. He didn't know why God had crossed their paths again. But maybe, just maybe, it was another step in this long, brutal journey toward healing.

The next day, Josiah sat down next to him at dinner.

Michael.

"Please leave me alone."

"Why?" asked Josiah.

"Because I don't deserve your conversation. You are probably in this situation because of me," he said.

"See, that's where you are wrong. I don't blame anyone for my situation. Everyone deserves another man's forgiveness. What makes you think that you don't?" asked Josiah.

Michael looked away, his eyes clouded with guilt and remorse. "I took something precious from you, something that can never be replaced," he whispered. "How can I ever be worthy of forgiveness?"

"You're right, you can't replace Marcus," Josiah said softly, his voice trembling with emotion. "But holding onto this guilt and refusing forgiveness helps no one. It doesn't bring my son back, and it doesn't allow you to heal. We both need to move forward."

With a stern voice, Josiah said "Look at me, son. "The Holy Scriptures state, 'And be ye kind one to another, tenderhearted, forgiving one another, even as God for Christ's sake hath forgiven you," said Josiah.

"I don't know if I can accept it from you or God," he said.

Josiah pleaded, "I did not create the moral code of right and wrong; we, as humans, attempt to adhere to the holy scriptures to the best of our abilities, as we are commanded to do so by God."

Michael hesitated to speak because he knew Josiah's words were valid. He had spent countless nights wrestling with his conscience, torn between his guilt and the possibility of redemption. The silence between them grew heavy, filled with unsaid words and unhealed wounds.

Finally, after several minutes of silence, Michael said, "You are right." I will accept your offering of forgiveness now. I must forgive myself, but I don't know how."

Josiah looked up from his food with a smile. He said, "If we confess our sins, he is faithful and just to forgive us our sins, and to cleanse us from all unrighteousness"-John 1:9 KJV.

Maybe you should start with a confession to God. Let God heal your guilt, and don't doubt that you can't recover from this. I'm going to continue to pray for you."

"Thank you," said Officer Johnson.

"You're welcome."

For the next few days, Josiah hoped their conversation had opened a door. But guilt is a stubborn chain, and sometimes the weight drags a man under before he can find his footing.

One night around 1:00 a.m., after working two shifts, Josiah was walking back to the shelter from the bus stop when flashing lights painted the street. EMS and police cars crowded the curb.

"What happened now?" Josiah thought, trying to enter, but an officer blocked him.

"Step aside," the officer said, guiding him next to three other men waiting to get in.

"What's going on?" Josiah asked.

"Somebody hung himself in the bathroom," one man answered grimly.

Josiah's heart sank. "No... we need to stick together when times get hard. We can't resort to self-harm," he said, lowering his head.

Moments later, EMS rolled a gurney past. A bump in the doorway shifted the white sheet, revealing the lifeless face beneath.

It was Officer Johnson.

Josiah's voice broke. "No, man! I thought you were doing better!" He tried to push forward, but the men beside him held him back.

"Do you know him, sir?" one of the officers asked.

"Yes. You should, too…. that's Officer Johnson."

"Oh, wow. That's the idiot who killed a victim during a school shooting," the officer scoffed.

Josiah clenched his fists, his spirit boiling with anger, but he refused to let rage speak for him. "Yes…. that's the man who killed my son during a school shooting. And you need to learn empathy and compassion for your fellow officer, regardless of his errors. He was a man…. with or without a uniform."

The officer rolled his eyes. "Sorry for your loss," he muttered before walking away.

Josiah stood frozen as they zipped the bag and loaded Johnson into the ambulance. Forgiveness hadn't saved him. But Josiah knew it was still worth giving because forgiveness was never just for the one receiving it. It was for the one who offered it, too.

# Chapter 21
## The Cost of Healing

Josiah sat on the edge of his bed, pulling on his worn sneakers. Morning light filtered through the thin curtains, casting a pale glow over the room. It had been weeks since Officer Johnson's death, but the image of the gurney, the white sheet, and the heavy thud in his chest when he recognized the man's face still lingered like an unwelcome shadow.

He didn't understand why he kept thinking about him. Maybe because forgiveness wasn't a one-time act, it was something you had to keep choosing, even when the person was gone.

Shaking the thought from his mind, he stood and grabbed his jacket. He had the evening shift at the 24-hour diner and needed a bus ticket from Mr. Richardson's office.

"Knock, knock," Josiah said, easing the door open.

"Come on in, Josiah," Mr. Richardson replied, glancing up from a stack of papers.

Josiah stepped inside. "I was wondering if you had an extra bus ticket."

Mr. Richardson reached into a drawer, then paused, studying him. "Yes, I do… but let me ask you something. How are you holding up? I know about Johnson. Word gets around here."

Josiah exhaled slowly. "I'm… managing. It's strange, though. You forgive a man, and then he's gone before either of you can figure out what to do with it."

Mr. Richardson leaned back in his chair. "Forgiveness isn't about what they do with it, Josiah. It's about what you do with it. You planted a seed in that man before he died. Whether he let it grow or not, that was between him and God. But you… You get to walk free."

Josiah swallowed hard. "Doesn't feel like freedom yet."

"It will," Mr. Richardson said, handing him the ticket. "Keep walking. God's not done with your story."

Josiah tucked the ticket into his pocket. "Thank you, sir."

The days turned into weeks, and Josiah's routine at the diner became a steady anchor in his life. The job wasn't glamorous... grease-stained aprons, late-night coffee orders, and mopping floors long after midnight, but it gave him purpose. Every check he received went into a small savings envelope tucked deep in his locker. He was determined to save enough for his apartment, a place where he could close the door and feel, even for a moment, like he belonged.

Months passed, and Josiah's dedication didn't go unnoticed. He showed up on time, took extra shifts when needed, and never complained. The regular customers began to greet him by name. The cook would sometimes slide him an extra pancake or burger during the slow hours, and his co-workers joked that he worked like he was training for a marathon.

One quiet afternoon, while wiping down tables, a regular customer lingered at his booth.

"How are you doing today?" the man asked.

Josiah smiled. "I've had better days, but I'm here."

The man nodded. "Josiah, you're always so diligent. Ever think about using that work ethic somewhere you could get ahead?"

"In what sense?" Josiah asked, curious.

"Construction," the man said.

Josiah's eyebrows lifted. "I used to work in construction years ago. Truth be told, I've wanted to get back to it."

The man grinned. "I might have an opportunity for you." He stood, pulling a folded bill and a business card from his pocket and placing it on the table. "I'll be in touch."

Josiah looked down, two crisp twenties. He stared after the man as he left, heart thudding. For the rest of the shift, he couldn't wipe the smile off his face. He wiped tables faster, greeted customers louder, and moved through the diner with a bounce in his step.

That night, walking back to the shelter, the city air felt different, less heavy, less cold. It wasn't just about the possibility of a job. It was about the feeling he had that allowed him to believe in it for a long time.

Hope.

Even if nothing came of it, Josiah knew something had shifted inside him. He was no longer just surviving. He was beginning to live again.

The cost of healing wasn't cheap. It had been paid in tears, in loss, in the hard work of forgiving the unforgivable. But as Josiah lay in his bunk that night, staring at the cracked ceiling, he realized he wasn't counting the cost anymore.

He was counting the steps forward.

# Chapter 22
## When Hope Breaks Ground

The diner had become Josiah's proving ground not glamorous, but steady. Every day he clocked in, scrubbed tables, balanced trays, and pocketed his wages. For months, he'd folded away each paycheck like a small investment in a better life. The faces of regulars became familiar, the clink of coffee cups a kind of music he could rely on.

But the saving came at a cost of long hours, sore feet, and rare moments of rest. On his first real day off in two weeks, he chose to rest in the park. The spring air felt like freedom. The sun warmed his shoulders, and the hum of distant traffic blended with the sound of children's laughter on the playground.

It had been years since he sat in the park without thinking of it as a shelter for the night. Today, it was simply a place to breathe. He unwrapped a turkey sandwich, taking slow bites, letting his mind wander.

"Hello."

The voice pulled him from his thoughts. Josiah turned his head and froze. Sitting beside him was the customer from the diner, the one who had promised to be in touch.

"Hello," Josiah replied cautiously, heart suddenly pounding. "How did you know where to find me?"

"I went by your place of work," the man said with an easy smile, "then stopped at the shelter. Mr. Richardson told me you usually hang out here."

Without wasting a moment, he continued, "Sorry I didn't come by sooner. I've been deep in preparations for a major project. But now I want you to apply for the construction manager position with my company."

Josiah blinked, unsure if he'd heard it right. "What's the name of the company?"

"I'm Peter Miller, with StoneBrook Development," the man said, extending his hand.

Josiah shook it firmly, still trying to process the moment.

Peter leaned in, his voice brimming with vision. "We're building a state-of-the-art community center and residential hall two conjoining buildings, with a capacity for 200 people. Right in the heart of the neighborhood."

Josiah's breath caught. "Wow. That's massive. Where?"

"Corner of Junction Avenue and 28th Street."

Josiah felt the words settle deep in his chest. He knew that corner. Knew the shadows, the cold nights, the feeling of hopelessness it once held. Now, someone wanted to put something beautiful there.

Peter slid a business card into his hand. "Your interview is in three days. Date, time, address…. all there. We need people who care about this city as much as I do."

Josiah stared at the card. "Thank you. Truly."

"If no one takes responsibility to change the community, then who will?" Peter said with a final nod before walking away.

Josiah sat there long after he'd gone, staring at the card like it was a key to another life. He could see it already, the walls going up, the rooms filling with laughter instead of despair. And for the first time in years, he felt not just hope, but purpose.

That night, he sat at a computer in the shelter's resource room, reading everything he could about StoneBrook Development. He practiced answers out loud, reviewed construction management trends, and even made a checklist of the questions he might ask. But sleep would not come every time he closed his eyes, he saw the building rising from the earth, and himself in a hard hat, giving orders.

On the day of the interview, Josiah wore the new suit he had bought with three weeks' worth of tips. At the StoneBrook offices, Peter greeted him warmly and introduced him to a panel of executives. For 45 minutes, they asked about his experience, his ideas for community design, and his vision for the project. Josiah answered each question with a calm confidence, weaving in his understanding of the community's needs.

When the interview ended, one of the executives said, "We'll be in touch."

The following week felt like a year. He kept working at the diner, trying not to read too much into every passing day without a call.

Then, one afternoon, Peter walked through the diner doors. The waitress found Josiah in the back stockroom. "Someone's here to see you," she said.

Josiah stepped out, his stomach in knots. "Whatever happens, you're still moving forward," he whispered to himself.

Peter stood up from his booth and extended his hand. "Josiah, congratulations. We're offering you the Construction Manager position. Every executive was impressed with your drive and your vision for the Kramer Project. Welcome to StoneBrook Development."

Josiah felt his throat tighten. For a moment, the diner noise faded, replaced by the sound of his heartbeat. He clasped Peter's hand. "Thank you. You won't regret it."

The next morning, Josiah turned in his resignation.

On his first day at StoneBrook, he stood at the edge of the construction site, hard hat in hand, staring at the ground where he once stood hungry, cold, and invisible. Now, he was here to help raise something that could keep someone else from experiencing that same darkness.

"I used to sleep steps from here," he thought. "Now, I'm building something that might save a life."

Over the next two years, Josiah poured himself into the work. He coordinated with architects, kept crews on schedule, and spent his Sundays back at the shelter serving meals alongside Mr. Richardson. His dedication earned him respect, friendships, and the quiet satisfaction of seeing hope take shape — one brick at a time.

As the Kramer Project neared completion, the community began to buzz with anticipation. For Josiah, it wasn't just a building. It was a monument to survival. A promise that no matter how far someone falls, the ground beneath them can still become a foundation.

# Chapter 23
## Better days, At Last

"Hi Josiah, are you ready for tonight's grand opening of the Kramer Project? I'm so excited for you and happy that you're also celebrating your second anniversary with the company," Peter's voice rang with pride through the phone.

Josiah smiled. "I greatly appreciate this opportunity, Peter. I believe the company is riding a new wave of success."

"It's because of you and your extraordinary vision in the construction industry. We're honored to have you aboard," Peter replied warmly. "See you tonight. The company car will pick you up in two hours."

The call ended.

In his modest two-bedroom apartment, Josiah stood still for a moment, letting the silence wrap around him. Then he moved to the closet and pulled out his black suit, the one he had carefully saved for nights like this. He polished his shoes until they caught the light, then fastened a deep purple-and-black bow tie with steady hands.

When he stepped to the mirror to straighten it, his reflection blurred with memory. Failures. Nights of hunger. Doubts that gnawed at him. Breakthroughs that seemed impossible. Prayers whispered in the dark when no one was listening but God.

"I can't believe it's been two years since I left that diner," he whispered, voice breaking. "Two years since Peter gave me a chance."

He sat on the edge of the bed, closing his eyes, taking a deep breath. A tear escaped, and he wiped it away with the back of his hand.

"I made it," he said aloud. "By God's grace... I made it."

A knock at the door broke the moment. The company driver stood there early but patient. Josiah shrugged on his jacket and stepped into the hallway with quiet determination. The sleek company car hummed to life, gliding through the city streets. When they turned the final corner, the sight of the Kramer Building rising against the evening sky nearly stole his breath. Lights blazed from its windows. A crowd stretched from the entrance to the curb.

Inside, champagne glasses clinked, and conversations swirled beneath towering ceilings. The air held the weight of celebration.

Peter spotted him instantly, breaking away from a group of sponsors.

"Josiah! It's a big night. Are you ready to give your speech?"

Josiah smiled, nerves tugging at him. "I'm ready."

Peter's grin widened. "Good. Let me introduce you to the people who helped make this dream possible."

As they began weaving through the crowd, Josiah's nerves stirred, but he reminded himself: this was part of his purpose. A few years ago, he had lost everything. And now, by the grace of God and the strength of perseverance, he was standing here, a builder of vision, hope, and second chances.

"Hello everyone, I would like for you all to meet the man behind this vision… Josiah Moore," said Peter. "Standing with him are Mrs. Celeste Greene, Mr. Evan White, and Mr. Jeremy Darrel, our top three contributors to this project.

They all shook Josiah's hand with enthusiasm and excitement.

"We are excited to meet you before you take the stage this evening," said Mrs. Greene. "What's your inspiration behind this massive and glorious creation?"

Before he spoke, Josiah swallowed the lump in his throat. "Well, this design is one of many, but this project is dear to my heart. The Kramer Project wasn't just about constructing buildings; it was about creating a sanctuary and a beacon of hope for the community. I don't want to ruin my speech, so I'm going to stop there."

They smiled.

Mr. White stated, "Fair enough," as they all walked into the main hall to begin the event.

Mr. Miller took center stage and sat as the rest of the guests took their seats. Moments later, the event coordinator introduced Peter Miller to the podium.

Everyone applauded as they stood.

"Thank you, everyone. Thank you," said Peter. He signaled with his hands for everyone to take their seats. "I am not the person of the hour, so I will get right to it. I want to introduce one of our top construction managers, who also designed the Kramer Project. Two years ago, I was sitting in a diner, eating lunch a few days a week. Each time I was there, I saw this person working diligently and thoroughly on every task given, without complaining. I knew then that he was someone StoneBrook Development needed.

"He opened my eyes to new levels in the construction world, and I embraced his eagerness to get back into it. He has an incredible story behind his brilliant and creative designs. Please give a warm welcome to the stage, Josiah Moore."

Everyone applauded as Josiah took the stage.

He shook Peter's hand as he approached him.

"You earned this, buddy," Peter whispered, giving him a slight hug.

Once at the podium, Josiah adjusted the microphone to fit his taller stature.

He took a deep breath before speaking. "Thank you, everyone, for coming out tonight to celebrate the Grand Opening of the Kramer Building. I want to thank God for allowing Peter to provide me with this incredible opportunity to showcase my vision in this project.

"This building is designed to reflect a person's life. As you see, the spiral staircases and the Calacatta Gold Marble flooring symbolize the good times in life. Yet the steel walls represent the strength and resilience that we must have during difficult times."

He paused while the crowd applauded.

"Thank you, everyone, for your gratitude," Josiah said.

He continued, voice steady yet reverent,

"Although this building is now a state-of-the-art center in the heart of our community... I...we.... cannot forget about what we used to call The Bird's Nest. On the streets, it was a shelter for people experiencing homelessness…. me included. For many, it was the only place to lay their heads. And for some… it became a grave."

He paused.

The air thickened with silence. A wave of empathy spread across the crowd.

Then, he went on.

"But today…. today is a better day. Today, we plant hope."

He looked toward Peter with a half-smile, then back to the audience.

"Mr. Miller told me, two years ago, while we sat on a park bench:

'If no one takes responsibility to change the community… then who will?'"

The crowd leaned in, moved by the memory.

"One project at a time," he said. "That's how transformation begins. It's in the seed, not the tree. We must allow our efforts to grow organically, faithfully into something greater than ourselves."

As he neared the end of his speech, he paused to adjust his bow tie. His voice deepened.

"In life, we all experience a little bit of Job's journey. His trials, his tribulations. But we must not lose faith in the process of waiting on God. I've soared, and I've suffocated… but I serve God not for what He gives, but for who He is."

His voice trembled as he lowered his head toward the microphone.

"And in the words of a man who went through more hell than I ever have…"

A breath. A beat.

He looked up, voice firm and clear:

*'And said, Naked came I out of my mother's womb, and naked shall I return thither:*

*The Lord gave, and the Lord hath taken away.*

*Blessed be the name of the Lord.' Job 1:21 KJV*

The crowd erupted in applause, some rising to their feet while others clapped through tears of joy.

He stepped away from the podium, tears filling his own eyes. Peter stood, wrapped him in a hug, and whispered, "You're going to be alright, brother."

Josiah nodded, overwhelmed. As he returned to his seat, he whispered to himself,

"I made it. Thank You, Lord."

Emotion flooded him. The tears he once held back were now free to flow. There was no shame, no fear. They traced his cheeks like rivers finally released.

He looked around the room, saw the emotion on others' faces, and knew:

His story, his suffering, his scars had a purpose.

Jewels gently touched Josiah's hand.

"I'm proud of you," she said softly.

He nodded.

Unbuckling his jacket with a deep sigh, Josiah leaned back in his chair and whispered once more,

"Lord… I almost gave up so many times… but I believed better days would come."

The storms persisted. However, I was able to maintain my faith through my lowest times in life and sought God first; then everything else fell into place.

As a result, I adjusted the way I walked.…

wet, broken, but still moving.

Still believing.

"To everything there is a season, and a time for every purpose under heaven."

Ecclesiastes 3:1 KJV

# Epilogue
## After The Storm

As the years unfolded, the bond between Jewels and Samantha deepened, woven together by love, laughter, and the quiet strength that only survivors truly understand. What began in the shadows of despair became a journey of transformational testimony that even the most broken paths can lead to purpose.

Jewels, once burdened by a past that nearly silenced her, walked boldly into a future shaped by faith. Her scars became symbols of survival. Her pain birthed compassion. And through it all, Samantha flourished a bright, radiant soul who carried no memory of the stall she had been found in, only the legacy of being chosen and cherished. Under Jewels' care, Samantha became a living reflection of what it means to grow in grace.

With time, she dreamed of becoming a nurse, someone who could help others heal, just as she had been nurtured. Her life, like her mother's, became a beacon of light for those still lost in the storm.

Miles away, Josiah Moore wrestled with a pain no parent should bear. The loss of his son, Marcus, during a school shooting had shattered his world. Yet in the ruins, Josiah found a calling to mentor young men, advocating for school safety, and quietly rebuilding his faith, one act of service at a time. Grief never left him, but it no longer controlled him. It became the soil where purpose took root.

When Jewels and Josiah's paths finally crossed, it wasn't a coincidence, it was providence. Two souls weathered by sorrow, stitched together by shared silence and resilience. In each other, they found understanding without explanation. Healing without pretense. Love, not as a fairy tale, but as a choice to believe again.

Their stories, so different in detail yet united in spirit proved a timeless truth: the storms may come, but they do not have the final say.

Together, they stood…. wounded, yes, but wiser. Not perfect, but purposeful. Their faith became the compass that guided them forward. With every prayer whispered in the dark and every scripture clung to in moments of weakness, they pressed on. Because they knew: it was never about escaping the storm, it was about learning to dance in the rain and trust God who calms the sea.

As we close these pages, may you remember storms shape us, but they do not define us. There is always hope. There is always faith. And there's God who walks with us through the fiercest winds.

Better days will come.

And yes, we will make it through the storms. God bless you.

## The End.

# Acknowledgments

To God, I'm grateful. Thank you.

To my family and friends,

Thank you for walking beside me on this journey. Your prayers, encouragement, and honest conversations have carried me through moments I wasn't sure I'd survive. Whether through a simple check-in, a shared laugh, or just your quiet presence, you reminded me that I was never alone. I am endlessly grateful for your friendship, your belief in my story, and your love that has never wavered.

To my current readers,

Thank you for choosing this book, for turning each page with your heart open. Whether you found healing, hope, or reflection in these words, know that your time and presence mean more than I could ever express. Your support gives this story its wings.

To my future readers,

Whenever you find these pages….months or even years from now, I hope they meet you in a meaningful way. I pray this story speaks to something inside you: a memory, a dream, a quiet hurt, or a silent hope. Know that these words were written for you, too.

May we continue to share light, grow through pain, and never stop believing in the beauty that follows the storm.

With all my heart, Kim

# About the Author

Kimberly Cummings is a passionate storyteller, community advocate, and believer in the power of faith and perseverance. With a background in criminal justice and leadership, she brings real-life depth to her writing, blending truth, pain, and healing into narratives that inspire and transform.

As a licensed childcare provider and former Director of Operations in logistics, Kimberly has spent years serving families and nurturing those around her. Her writing reflects her dedication to restoration, justice, and the human spirit's resilience.

Through the Storms is one of many works that reflect her heart for change and her desire to encourage others through storytelling. She continues to write from a place of honesty, truth, and hope, with the prayer that her words reach those who need them most.

Connect with her via email: scratchpadcreate@gmail.com or http://www.kimberlycummingsauthor.com